THE SURVIVALIST 5
THE WEB

John Rourke looked at the Rolex; the exterior of the crystal was steamed so he smudged it away with his right glove, then studied the time. It was eight-thirty.

He leaned against the pine trunk, staring down into the valley, the wind behind him now, the sweater pulled down from covering his head, his leather jacket unzipped and wide open. The Bushnell Armored 8X30s focused under his hands as he swept them across the valley floor. A town – a perfect town, nothing changed. A blue-grass band was playing in the town square, strains of the music barely audible in the distance; children played behind a crowd of spectators surrounding the band; a car moved along the far side of the town, its lights setting a pattern of zigzags in the shadows where the streetlights didn't hit.

For an instant only, Rourke questioned his own sanity, then dismissed the idea.

He was sane; it was what he saw that wasn't sane.

He and Natalia and Paul had often talked about it – a world gone mad; but beneath him now, on the valley floor, was a world that hadn't changed. Was that madness?

*The Survivalist series by Jerry Ahern,
published by New English Library:*

1: Total War
2: The Nightmare Begins
3: The Quest
4: The Doomsayer
5: The Web
6: The Savage Horde
7: The Prophet
8: The End Is Coming
9: Earth Fire
10: The Awakening
11: The Reprisal
12: The Rebellion
13: Pursuit

The Survivalist 5
The Web

Jerry Ahern

NEW ENGLISH LIBRARY
Hodder and Stoughton

First published in the USA in 1983
by Kensington Publishing Corp.
Copyright © 1983 by Jerry Ahern

First NEL Paperback Edition 1984
Fifth impression 1987

Printed and bound in Great
Britain for Hodder and Stoughton
Paperbacks, a division of
Hodder and Stoughton Limited,
Mill Road, Dunton Green,
Sevenoaks, Kent, TN13 2YA.
(Editorial Office: 47 Bedford
Square, London WC1B 3DP) by
Robert Hartnoll (1985) Limited,
Bodmin, Cornwall.

ISBN 0-450-05722-4

For all the readers who patiently waited this long. In a world gone mad, the adventures of John Rourke, Natalia, Paul, Sarah, and the children continue.

Prologue

John Rourke stood in the rain. He'd landed the Beech-craft because the plane had been almost out of fuel. As best he'd been able to judge from the maps, the plane was about twenty-five miles from Chambers and U.S. II headquarters.

Paul was sitting in the plane, talking to his parents; the pilot had gone to find some kind of transportation. The radio wasn't working well, too much static.

Beside Rourke stood Maj. Natalia Tiemerovna. "The truce will be over soon, John; it is over now, I think."

"At least it showed we're still human beings, didn't it?" Rourke said quietly, his left hand cupped over his dark tobacco cigar, his right arm around Natalia.

"You will go on looking?" she asked.

"Yes."

"Where do you plan to go?"

"The Carolinas, maybe Georgia by Savannah. She was likely headed that way."

"I hope you find her—and the children."

Rourke looked at the Russian woman. Rain water streamed down her face—and his. "Thank you, Natalia."

The woman smiled, then lowered her eyes. She stood beside Rourke in the pouring rain.

Chapter 1

"I just damned well can't order my men to fire on Americans to save a Russian agent, Rourke—no matter how much she's helped us!"

Rourke glanced at Reed, then snatched a Mossberg 500 ATP6P riot pump from one of Reed's men. "Nobody has to order me," he whispered, squinting hard against the sunshine as he tromboned the shotgun and shouldered it.

"Rourke!"

"Leave it!" Rourke ordered, not looking at Reed as the Army Intelligence captain spoke.

The crowd of men and women—civilians, mostly—was advancing, rifles, shotguns, clubs, and knives of every description in their hands. A woman screamed from the crowd, "Give us that Commie bitch—now!"

Rourke snapped the muzzle of the riot shotgun down fast, firing, pumping, then firing again, skipping the pellets of double-O buck across the tarred surface of the runway-access road, the pellets at most ricocheting upward against the shins of the lead ranks of the mob. The mob fell back a few yards. Rourke worked the tang-mounted safety after tromboning another round into the chamber, then handed the shotgun to Reed. "That's called riot control—ever hear of it?"

Rourke didn't wait for an answer, extending his hand; Reed took it. "You didn't get weather from the tower."

"That's all right—couldn't be hotter up there than it is here." Rourke nodded toward the mob. They were advancing again. Reed shouldered the pump and worked the safety, then fired into the runway surface, the roughly thirty-caliber pellets skipping toward the rioters. "See—works just great. About two more times, and the braver ones are gonna figure you're trying too hard not to kill 'em—then they're going to rush you. Let 'em past; we'll be airborne."

"Rourke?"

"Yeah—I know. Good luck." Rourke nodded fast, then took off in a dead run behind the dozen or so armed U.S. II troopers and toward the pickup truck.

"He's gonna make a break for it with the Russian girl!" an angry voice shouted from the crowd behind him. Rourke hoped the anonymous voice was right.

He reached the truck, jumping aboard, the door not closed as he worked the key. The ignition fired; his right fist locked on the floor-mounted gearshift. His left foot popped the clutch; the dark tobacco cigar moved across the clenched tight teeth and settled in the left corner of his mouth as the truck lurched ahead. The truck door slammed itself, the mirror vibrating as Rourke studied it. The mob had closed with Reed's men, closed with them sooner than Rourke had expected, and had passed them. There was sporadic gunfire, and behind the truck now, Rourke could see the first ragged ranks of the mob—running after him toward the airfield.

Far ahead, through the cracked glass of the Ford's windshield, he could see the light cargo plane, the twin props still not whirring. Rourke hammered his left fist down hard on the vintage truck's horn button, again and again.

He could see a figure—Rubenstein?—running from the starboard wing around the nose of the aircraft. Natalia would be at the controls. "Shit!"

Rourke stomped the clutch down hard, working the gas pedal as well, double-clutching as he upshifted, the truck's gears grinding. The vehicle bumped, then lurched ahead.

He glanced to his left—something, a sixth sense, making him do it. Hearing anything over the roar of his truck's engine, the gunfire, and the shouts of the mob from behind was impossible. From his left were coming two pickup trucks, armed men in the backs of each vehicle—rifles, shotguns, handguns, axes—and blood in their collective eye.

He shook his head, almost in disbelief. Three days earlier, Natalia had been rescuing their wives and babies, putting them aboard the planes of the evacuation fleet in Florida. But now—none of that mattered. She was Russian, and the Russians had started World War III, destroyed much of the United States, invaded American shores. Natalia was Russian. It didn't matter who she was, just what. Rourke felt the corners of his mouth downturning. "Ignorant bastards!" Rourke snarled as he glanced again at the two pickup trucks. They were closing fast, gunfire now being leveled at him from the beds of the trucks. The West Coast mirror on the right-hand side of the vintage Ford pickup he drove shattered under the impact of a slug.

Rourke reached under his left armpit, snatching at one of the twin Detonics stainless .45s he carried in the

11

double Alessi shoulder rig. He aimed the pistol as his thumb cocked the hammer, then turned his face away from the passenger-side window, firing, as the shattering outward of the passenger-side glass and the roar of the .185-grain JHP in the confined space all came together to make his ears ring. He looked toward the passenger side; the nearest of the two trucks swung away. He fired the Detonics again; this time, the glass of his borrowed truck not partially deflecting the bullet, his bullet hammered into the front windshield of the nearest of the pursuers.

Rourke glanced to his left, seeing behind him through the driver's-side window the pursuing mob. The mob split, a wing of it running diagonally from the access road toward the field, to cut him off or to reach the airplane ahead of him—he couldn't be sure which.

Rourke glanced to his right. A wooden fence was all that separated him from the grassy area leading toward the field. He cut the wheel hard right, the cocked and locked Detonics secured under his right thigh as he aimed the pickup truck toward the fence. One of the pursuing trucks, the one with the shot-out windshield, was coming for him broadside. Rourke grabbed up the Detonics again, firing. The pursuing truck swerved hard right through the wooden fence, almost in perfect simultaneity with the truck Rourke drove.

Behind him now, Rourke could see the second truck, coming up fast as it punched through the fence. Some of the fence slats, caught up in its front bumper, broke away as the truck, a Chevy, bounced and jarred across the uneven ground. Rourke upped the safety on his Detonics again, hammering down the gas pedal and shifting down into third, releasing the pedal and stomping the accelerator as he made the change. The Ford slowed, but took the bumps better. There were perhaps a thousand yards to go toward the airfield tarmac itself.

The pickup with the shot-out windshield was coming—fast, too fast for control. The riflemen and shotgunners, bouncing visibly in the bed as the truck slowed, fired. Rifle bullets and shotgun slugs pinged uselessly off the body of Rourke's truck.

Rourke fired the Detonics .45 again, really at nothing, since aimed fire was useless with the truck he drove bouncing and jarring as it did. But this time the pickup truck, a Dodge, didn't fall back.

"Hell," Rourke rasped, stomping the clutch, running the gas pedal hard down as he upshifted, easing the gas pressure, then increasing it again. The Ford lurched ahead.

In the rear-view mirror, Rourke could see the Chevy—almost even with the rear end of his truck now, a man leaning out of its passenger-side door, jumping. Rourke tried swerving away in time, but was boxed in.

The man, a pistol in his right hand now, was unsteadily standing in the bed of Rourke's pickup. Rourke tried cutting the wheel hard right, to throw the man off, but the Dodge with the shattered windshield was flanking him, fenders touching, boxing him in again. Rourke cut the wheel hard left, but the second pickup, the Chevy, had blocked him there as well. The man standing shakily behind him was raising his pistol, to fire through the rear window. "Try this," Rourke snapped, stomping hard on the brakes. The pickup truck lurched to a ragged halt; the man's pistol discharged, the man himself sailing forward, disappearing from Rourke's view over the cab of the pickup and reappearing crashing onto the hood. Rourke threw the stick into reverse, the truck's gearbox grinding. Rourke's right foot hammered down on the gas pedal. The Chevy was already twenty yards ahead of him; the Dodge, customized and massive, locked beside him. There was a tearing sound, metal against metal. The right side of Rourke's truck locked into the left rear wheel well of the Dodge with the shot-out windshield. Rourke stomped the clutch again, throwing into first, then hammering down the gas pedal. There were more tearing sounds; then his truck lurched ahead. The Ford's bumper twisted upward suddenly, protruding over the hood as Rourke stomped the clutch again, into second with the gearbox, his foot barely leaving the gas pedal.

The Chevy was wheeling a sharp right, trying to cut Rourke off. The man from the bed of Rourke's pickup, who had been thrown to the ground an instant earlier, got unsteadily to his feet. Rourke cut his wheel sharp to the left, barely missing him, then hard to the right. The Chevy still trying to cut him off.

The first truck, its windshield all but gone now, was right behind him. Rourke stomped his brake pedal, wrenching the stick back into reverse. There was a massive hitchball on the rear end of the Ford and Rourke aimed it blindly now toward the grillwork of the Dodge behind him. There was a crashing, crunching sound, and Rourke braced himself against the wheel as the Ford impacted. Rourke stomped the clutch, then worked the stick into first and gave the Ford the gas. There was a groaning sound. His truck stalled a little, then ripped free. Behind him, in the rear-view, as he upshifted to second, he could see the front bumper and part of the Dodge's grill—twisted and wrecked.

The Chevy was alongside him again. Rourke cut his wheel sharp right, impacting the right fender against the left fender of the other truck, then cutting back away, keeping the wheel in a sharp left, circling back over the ground they had just traversed, the Chevy still coming.

Gunfire—an assault rifle, the burst long, too long. The rear windshield of the truck Rourke drove shattered, the rear-view mirror was shot out, too, as bullets passed through the opening in the glass behind him and hammered against the front windshield from the inside.

Rourke ducked his head down. Under the impact of more slugs, the gas gauge shattered, the steering wheel chipped—too near his fingers.

"Hell," he rasped, cutting the wheel into a hard left, then a hard right, then a hard left again, zigzagging as the Chevy kept coming and the assault-rifle fire as well. He cut the wheel sharp right and worked the emergency brake, locking the rear wheels. The truck skidded into a flick turn, almost overending.

He was aimed the right way now, his left hand snatching for the second Detonics pistol as he released the emergency brake. He rammed the transmission into first, into second, then into third, his feet working as if they rode a balance beam, his right hand stirring the transmission. The Chevy was coming at him—dead-on.

"Play chicken with me!" he snarled. Ramming the Detonics pistol out the driver's-side window, his thumb jerked the hammer back, his first finger started the squeeze.

One round, then a second—the enemy truck's windshield gone with two hits. Two more shots—one headlight and maybe a puncture to the radiator. The truck was still coming.

One round—the driver's-side West Coast mirror. The truck wasn't swerving, coming at Rourke like a rival knight in a tournament. The gap between them was less than twenty yards. Rourke fired the last round from the pistol. The driver of the Chevy threw his hands up to his face; the pickup swerved left and right. Rourke stomped down on the Ford's clutch, wrenching the stick into second as he double-clutched, working the emergency brake again, cutting the wheel in a sharp left, then releasing the brake and stomping the gas. The Ford fishtailed under him, bounced up, and drove over a hummock of ground, airborne for a split second. He could feel the suspension of gravity in the instant that it happened, feel it in the pit of his stomach. The truck hit hard, Rourke fighting the wheel to control it. He stomped the clutch, wrenching the stick into third, revving his way out of the fishtail, accelerating, the engine moaning in front of him, the cab vibrating, shards of glass tinkling to the floor of the cab as the air of the truck's slipstream pressured his bullet-shattered windshield.

The twin-engine light cargo plane was just ahead of him again, this time barely a hundred yards away.

Rourke upshifted into fourth as he hit the runway tarmac. The truck skidded—the treads of the tires would be packed with clay and dirt, he knew. The Ford fishtailed again, then straightened out as Rourke started downshifting, braking at the same time. The toes of his right foot worked the gas pedal, his heel worked the brake, his left foot worked the clutch. The truck was skidding, and Rourke cut the wheel hard right, riding into the skid as he braked. The truck lurched once, then stopped.

Rourke wrenched open the driver's-side door; shards of windshield glass showered down on him from the dashboard.

Natalia's face—her brilliantly blue eyes framed in the bell of her almost black, past-shoulder-length hair—was visible through the pilot's-side storm window. Rubenstein, framed in the open cargo bay, pushed his glasses back off the bridge of his nose as he shouted, "John—what the hell—"

Rourke cut the younger man off. "Paul—get everything nailed down fast, if it isn't already." Without another word, Rourke ran toward the wing stem and jumped for it, the pilot's-side door opening under his right hand. Natalia was seated behind the controls.

"Move over," Rourke ordered her.

Her blue eyes were wide—not terror, but recognition, he thought; recognition, perhaps, of the insanity of what was happening. "They want me—don't they, John? To kill me."

"They'd try killing the Virgin Mother right now if she were a Russian. Move over I said." She slipped out of the pilot's seat as Rourke slid down behind the controls.

He checked the parking brake. "You through preflighting?"

"Yes," she answered, sounding lifeless. "Everything's fine—ready."

He didn't say anything. Through the pilot's-side storm window, he could see at least three dozen armed men running across the field; and one of the trucks—the Chevy—was rolling again. "Damn it," he rasped to himself; then he shouted, "Paul! Get that cargo hold buttoned up. Then get up here with a gun!"

"You can't ask him to shoot those people—for me," Natalia almost whispered.

Not looking at her as he spoke, Rourke ran a visual check of the avionics. "You listen to me—and good. Rus-

17

sian or whatever—I don't even have the words for it. Maybe Paul would. But the three of us—we've come this far together. And that means something." Rourke checked the oxygen. The cowl flap switches were open. He set the fuel selector valves to "main," the induction air system to "filtered." Visually, he surveyed the circuit breakers and switches; there wasn't time for a full check. He flipped the battery switch to "on."

Glancing at the main and auxiliary fuel indicators, he started throttling open, the prop controls at low pitch. He adjusted the mixture controls—full rich. He checked the auxiliary fuel pump; it was registering high. He switched it off.

Glancing out the cockpit storm window again, he hit the magneto/start switch.

"Paul—up here with a gun!"

Already, Rourke was exercising the props, watching the rpms build. He throttled out, checked the magneto variances, throttled again. "Little late to ask—the wheel chocks gone?"

"Yes." She smiled, laughing for an instant.

Rourke nodded, feathering the props, the mob less than a hundred yards away now, the Chevy pickup closing fast. There was no glass in its windshield, and men, packed in its truck bed, were firing rifles and shotguns.

"Paul!"

"Right here."

Rourke glanced behind him; the younger man held Rourke's CAR-15 in his right hand; his left was pushing the wire-rimmed glasses back from the bridge of his nose.

"Put a few shots out the storm window," Rourke ordered. Then, concentrating on getting airborne, he ignored the mob. Trim tabs, flaps—he set them for take-off.

He released the parking brake. "Let's get the hell out of here," Rourke almost whispered.

"Brace yourself Paul—and keep shooting." For the last ten seconds, pieces of hot brass had pelted his neck and shoulders—Rubenstein firing the Colt assault rifle toward the mob. The younger man stood almost directly behind him.

Rourke glanced at the oil temperature, then rasped half to himself, "Full throttle—God help us."

He checked the fuel altitude setting as he released the brake. The aircraft was already accelerating. "Buckle up, Paul," Rourke ordered. More of the hot brass pelted him, then suddenly stopped. Above the roaring of the engines there were sounds now of gunfire from the field, of projectiles pinging against the aircraft fuselage.

"What if they hit something?" Rubenstein called out.

"Then we maybe die," Rourke answered emotionlessly. He checked his speed; through the cockpit windshield the runway was blurring under him now. The Chevy still came, gunfire pouring from it, the mob suddenly far behind. The pickup was closing fast.

Rourke checked his speed—not quite airspeed yet. The far chain-link fence at the end of the airfield was coming up—too fast. More gunfire; the pilot's side window spiderwebbed beside Rourke's head as a bullet impacted against the glass.

And Rubenstein was firing again as well, having ignored Rourke's admonition to strap in. The Chevy swerved; one of the men in the truck bed fell out onto the runway surface. The gunfire was heavier now, sparks flying as Rubenstein's .223 slugs hammered against the pickup truck's body.

"Hang on!" Rourke worked the throttles to maximum, starting to pull up on the controls—a hundred yards, fifty yards, twenty-five yards, the nose starting up. Rourke punched the landing-gear-retraction switch, and as they cleared the fence top, the pelting of hot brass against his neck subsided, Rubenstein's gunfire having ceased.

"Thank God." Rubenstein sighed.

"Hmmm." Rourke worked the controls, opening his cowl flaps, trying to climb, gunfire still echoing from below and behind them.

He checked his airspeed—not good enough—then began playing the cowl flaps and the fuel flow. The airspeed was rising. As Rourke banked the aircraft hard to port, Natalia leaned half out of her seat, across his right shoulder, Rubenstein to his left. The Chevy, now far below them, had stopped. The men with rifles and shotguns in the pickup's bed were now minuscule specks, more a curiosity than a threat.

"Can I breathe now?" Paul Rubenstein asked.

Smiling, Rourke checked the oxygen system on the control panel, then nodded. "Yeah." Rourke decided to breathe, too. . . .

The controls vibrated under Rourke's hands as he sat alone in the cockpit. Natalia had gone aft with Paul, to help him resecure some of the gear that had jarred loose during the overly rapid takeoff. The airfield tower had given him the weather—generally good, moderate winds, perhaps a few thunderheads, but at low elevations and unlikely to be encountered. Rourke looked below the craft now, its shadow stark and black against the emptiness that he saw. That expanse of wasteland had once been the Mississippi Delta region. Now, like the rest of the Mississippi valley from where New Orleans had been to its farthest extent north, the ground was a radioactive desert.

The Night of the War . . . Rourke could not forget it, and at last lighting the small dark tobacco cigar that he'd had clenched in his teeth for nearly an hour, he thought more about it. The anger of the men and women in the mob back at the airfield, even the reluctance of Reed to risk an American life to save a Russian life, no matter how valuable, how good—it had all started then, on the Night of the War.

The global fencing—the saber rattling—had ended long before anyone had realized and the nuclear weapons had been unsheathed and ready. The death . . . all of the death in that one night, millions of lives lost. The pounding of nuclear weapons, which here, below him, had produced an irradiated vastness that would be uninhabitable for perhaps as long as a quarter-million years, had struck along the San Andreas fault line and brought about the feared megaquakes—but far worse than anyone, save the most wild speculator, had ever imagined. Much of California and the West Coast had fallen into the sea—more millions of deaths. The Soviet Army—the Soviet Union itself—was nearly as crippled as was what had been the United States. The invading Soviet Army, headquartered in neutron-bombed Chicago, had set up outposts in surviving major American cities and industrial and agricultural regions, outposts that not only contended with the growing wave of American resistance, but with the Brigand problem. Rourke felt a smile cross his lips as he exhaled the gray smoke of his cigar. Something in common with the self-styled conquerors—the Brigand warfare, the pillaging, the slaughters.

For it was after the war that both the best and worst of humanity had risen to the fore. The best—Paul, certainly. The young Jewish New Yorker had never ridden anything more challenging than a desk, never fought anything tougher than an editorial deadline. Now, in the few short weeks since the world had forever changed, Rubenstein had forever changed as well. Tough, good with a gun, as at home on a motorcycle as he had been in a desk chair. Even in the short period of time that had elapsed, Rourke had noted the definition of his musculature, and the different set to the eyes he continuously shielded behind wire-rimmed glasses. The wonder, the excitement, were all there as they had been from the first with each new challenge; but there was something else—a pride, a determination derived just from having survived, from having fought, from having surmounted obstacles. In those few short weeks, Rubenstein had grown to be the best friend Rourke felt he had ever had—like a brother, Rourke thought, feeling himself smile again. An only child, he had never been blessed with a natural brother. But now at least he had one.

And Natalia—the magic of her eyes, the beauty that he would have felt hopelessly inadequate to describe had the need arisen to do so. Rourke had first met her before the war—a brief, chance meeting in Latin America when she had worked with her now-dead husband, Vladmir Karamatsov. Rourke had been a CIA covert operations officer; Karamatsov had been the same thing—but for KGB, the Soviet Committee for State Security. And Natalia had been Karamatsov's agent. Then, after the war, there was the staggering coincidence of finding her, dying, wandering the west Texas desert, herself the victim of Brigand attack. The feelings that had grown between him and the Russian woman, despite her loyalty to her country, despite her job in the KGB, despite her uncle—General Varakov, who was the supreme Soviet commander for the North American Army of Occupation. "Insane," he murmured to himself.

And then another chance meeting. Rourke had been pursuing the trail of his wife, Sarah, and the children, lost to him on the Night of the War. Rourke let out a deep breath, feeling the tendons in his neck tightening with the thoughts. "Sarah," he heard himself whisper. The meeting—the meeting with the girl named Sissy; the seismological research data she had carried regarding the development of an artificial fault line during the bombing, something that would reduplicate the horror of the megaquakes that had destroyed the West Coast, but would instead now sever the Florida peninsula from the mainland.

For all the destruction and the death, it had proven again that there still remained some humanity, some commonality of species. For with President Chambers of U.S. II and General Varakov, a Soviet-U.S. II truce had been struck to effect the evacuation of peninsular Florida in the hope of saving human lives.

The job finished, the truce had ended and a state of war existed once again.

Rourke shook his head. War. Sarah had always labeled his study of survivalism, his knowledge of weapons—all of it—as a preoccupation with gloom and doom, a fascination with the unthinkable. It had torn at their marriage, separated them, and now, despite the fact that they had promised each other to try again for the sake of

Michael and Annie, for the sake of the love he and Sarah had always felt for each other, it was war that had finally separated them.

Rourke remembered it; he hadn't wanted to leave, to give the lecture to be delivered in Canada. Hypothermia—the effects of cold. The world situation had been already tense; but Sarah had insisted, so she could get herself together, to try again with him. It had been there, in Canada, that Rourke had at last learned of the gravity of the situation rapidly developing between the United States and the Soviet Union. He had been aboard an aircraft nearly ready to land in Atlanta, near his farm in northeastern Georgia, when he had heard over the pilot's PA system that the first missiles had been launched. Then that night—the night that had lasted, it seemed, forever, and nothing ever the same afterward.

He shivered from the memories: the crash after the plane had been diverted westward, the struggle to survive afterward with the injured passengers, the uselessness of his skills as a doctor to the burn victims in Albuquerque—then the slaughter of the passengers by the Brigands. "Brigands," he murmured. He glanced at his watch; the black-faced Rolex Submariner showed that he had been lost in his reverie for at least ten minutes, perhaps longer. He checked the instruments, then the ground below him—now a nuclear desert, a no man's land where once millions had lived, worked, tilled the soil—nothing now. Not a living tree, or a blade of grass that wasn't brown or black.

His cigar was gone from his teeth and he checked the ashtray, realizing he'd extinguished it. Rourke shook his head, silent—tired. . . .

Chapter 2

Reed started to stub out his cigarette, but didn't. Cigarettes were getting harder to find. He kept smoking it, then looked up across the littered table from his cup of coffee. "What, Corporal?"

"Captain, your pal, Dr. Rourke—he's gonna have trouble, sir."

"He had trouble—remember? Hell of a lot of good we were to stop it." He looked back at the cigarette and noticed that the skin of his first and second fingers was stained dark orange. Reed wondered what the stuff in the cigarettes did to his lungs. He shrugged and took another drag; then through a mouthful of smoke, he said, "What kind of trouble? He's got a radio. We can contact him."

"A storm system—it just moved in, like it was out of nowhere, sir."

"He's a fine pilot. He'll fly over it," Reed answered, dismissing the problem.

"But, Captain?"

Reed looked up at the red-haired young woman again. "What, Corporal?"

"You don't understand, sir," she insisted. "See. It's a massive winter storm system—it was just there. You

25

know the weather's been crazy—"

"Winter storm system? Have you weather people ever figured out you can learn a hell of a lot by just looking out the damn window?" Reed checked his wrist watch, thinking of Rourke for an instant and envying Rourke the Rolex he habitually wore. "An hour ago it was in the sixties—snowstorm?"

"Sir . . . please," the red-haired woman said.

"Yeah." He nodded, tired from going more than a day without sleep. Standing slowly, he stubbed out the cigarette and looked around the place—some officer's club, he thought. One lousy window. He walked across the room, lurching a little because of sitting so long in one chair, tired. He staggered against the back of a chair. A Marine lieutenant started to his feet, saw Reed, then looked noncommittal. Reed shrugged it off, reaching the window. "I need a good couple hours sleep, Corporal."

"Yes, sir." The red-haired woman nodded.

Reed pulled back the heavy curtain. Staring outside, he whispered, "Holy shit!" He judged the depth, at least four inches of snow; a heavy wind was blowing what had fallen back into the air. Drifts were mounting against the tires of a jeep outside by the walkway.

"Yes, sir. That's it, sir," the red-haired woman echoed.

Reed looked at her. "It's impossible! It was like spring a few—"

He looked back out the window. It was no longer like spring.

Chapter 3

The sleet was coming in torrents now. Sarah huddled beside the children under the overhang of rocks, a pine bracken to her right, as she stared down into the valley. The pines made a natural windbreak for herself, Michael, Annie, and the horses.

Across her lap, resting on her blue-jeaned thighs instead of the children's heads, was the AR-15—the one modified to fire fully automatically when she put the selector at the right setting, the one almost used to kill her the morning after the Night of the War, the one she'd taken from the dead Brigand and used to shoot out the glass window in the basement of her house in order to set off the confined natural gas there after the gas lines had begun filling the house following the bombing—to blow up her own home and the men inside it who had tried to rob, to kill, to rape.

Priorities were odd, she thought, as she raised her left hand from Annie's chest where it had rested and tugged the blue-and-white bandanna from her own hair. Before the Night of the War—rape, it would have been a top priority. But now losing things had somehow become unconsciously more important as she considered life.

27

Rape would be a horror—but it could be overcome. Death—it might well be more than expected. But to be robbed, deprived of food or horses or weapons with which to fight—this was worse than death, and rape of the spirit more foul than any rape of the body.

She looked to her right. Michael was sleeping, his body swathed—like Annie's—in blankets against the bizarre and sudden cold. Michael would be turning eight soon, and already he had murdered a man—a Brigand who had tried to rape her.

She studied his face. It was John's face, but younger, though appearing no less troubled. She could see the faint tracing of lines which in adulthood would duplicate the lines in the face of his father. She could see the set of his chin. She thought of his father's face, the quiet, the resoluteness, the firmness. She found herself missing that—the steadiness with which John Rourke's infrequent life at home had provided her.

She watched the valley, the impromptu-appearing Brigand encampment there, pickup trucks sheltered with tarps, and motorcycles, these, too, covered—covered better than her children.

The sleet had begun to stream down from the gray-blue skies more than two hours earlier. Sarah had quickly led the horses—the children mounted on her husband's horse, Sam—up and away from the low valley now below her. For she had seen the Brigands already, heard their vehicles, their laughter and shouts, felt the fear they always made her feel. She had tethered Sam and Tildie, then wrapped the children in their blankets and in hers as well. Now she sat, huddled in an incongruously feminine woolen jacket, on two saddle blankets spread over the bare rock. She was freezing with the cold.

She looked away from the Brigand camp below. There were perhaps a dozen of them, a small force by comparison to some she had seen, almost encountered. She looked instead at the faces of Michael and Annie, trying to remember the last time she had seen either child really play. Not on the offshore island where they had hidden from the Soviet troops in Savannah. But at the Mulliner farm. The children had played there. Mary Mulliner had . . .

Sarah looked down at herself, the rifle across her blue-jeaned thighs. She had worn a dress at the Mulliner farm much of the time, slept in a warm bed at night, worn a nightgown. The children—they had run with the dog Mary kept, forgetting the times they'd run from wild dogs.

There was Mary's son; he fought with the Resistance against the Soviet Army. And the Resistance would have ways of reaching Army Intelligence. If John had gone to Texas near the Louisiana border, as the intelligence man in Savannah had told her, then Mary's son would have a way of contacting John, of letting him know. . . .

She hugged her knees close to her chin, watching the faces of her children; there was little happines in them. But there would be happiness again.

Suddenly, desperately, she wanted to be rid of her rifle, rid of her war of nerves with every strange sound in the night, rid of the worry.

Her eyes closed, she imagined herself, in her borrowed dress, living at the Mulliner farm, living like a person again.

She opened her eyes, gazing down at the valley. The Brigands—they would rob, kill, rape her if they guessed her presence. But they would leave eventually. If she turned north, despite the storm, she could reach Mt. Eagle, Tennessee in a matter of days. Texas was farther away than that—farther away.

Sarah Rourke closed her eyes again, trying to forget the Brigands and see the faces of her children, playing. But instead, in her mind all she could see was the face of her husband, John Thomas Rourke.

Chapter 4

"These are all the reports, Catherine; there is nothing fresh from the radio room?"

"There is nothing fresh from the communications center, Comrade General," the young woman answered him.

Varakov looked up from the sheaves of open file folders littering his desk, into Catherine's young eyes. "I love the way, girl, that you correct me—communications center it is, then." He slammed his fist—heavily and slowly—down on the last of the file folders he'd opened, then stared at the desk. Nothing concretely showed that Natalia, his niece, was safe.

"Comrade General?"

Ishmael Varakov looked up at the young secretary again. "Yes, I worry over Major Tiemerovna. I would worry over you, too, I think because I tend to feel like everyone's father. When one reaches my age, girl, he feels that way. You may, too, someday. Now leave me. You have,"—he looked at the watch on his tree limb-sized wrist—"you have gone with little sleep for three days, I think. Each time that I call you, you are here—and that is impossible if you go off duty to sleep. You will

31

be of no use as my secretary in the hospital. You are off duty for twenty-four hours. Go and sleep, Catherine." Varakov felt mildly proud of himself for remembering her name.

"But, Com—"

She didn't finish what she started to say, and as he looked at her, she averted her eyes downward, her long-fingered hands with the plain nails clutching the steno pad in front of her at the waistline of her skirt.

"You mean well—to help me. It is more than you do your duty; you are a friend, Catherine. And that is too valuable a commodity to waste. Sleep—I order you that. You will obey me."

She stood very straightly—too straight to be comfortable, Varakov thought—then answered him. "Yes, Comrade General."

"You are a good person—go." He looked down at his desk, hearing her too-low heels clicking across the museum floor. He looked up after her once; her skirt was still too long. He would mention it again to Natalia to tell the girl. It would be better for a woman to mention such a thing. "Natalia," he whispered.

Was she alive?

As best he could piece together from the fragmentary reports of the Florida evacuation, Natalia had been with Rourke, working to save the last of the refugees near Miami. The last Soviet report had indicated seeing Natalia and Rourke on the field with a group of older American men and women. Minutes after that, according to high-altitude observation planes, the final shock wave had apparently taken place, the Florida peninsula had broken..up and—

Varakov hammered his fist down on the desk, stood

32

up, awkwardly leaned across the desk in his office-without-walls, and stuffed his white-stockinged feet into his shoes.

His uniform blouse still open, he walked toward the main hall of the museum, his feet hurting as they always did when he walked. "The soldier's curse," he murmured, stopping not quite halfway across the main hall to look at the figures of the mastodons, fighting. He watched them.

How huge they were, how powerful—all once, long ago.

He snorted, shaking his head, still standing there, not walking. She should be safe—she had been with—

"Comrade General!"

Varakov turned, staring. A man was standing on the mezzanine balcony, staring down either at him or at the figures of the mastodons. "Comrade General!"

The man was already starting down the gently winding staircase to Varakov's left, starting toward him, moving with the grace of an athlete, taking the stairs effortlessly in his comparative youth.

Varakov heard his own lips murmur, "Colonel Nehemiah Rozhdestvenskiy—aagh—"

"I was looking for you, Comrade General!"

Varakov did not answer; the man was still halfway across the length of the natural history museum's great hall and Varakov would not shout.

Rozhdestvenskiy slowed his easy jog, stopping and standing at attention, a boyish smile across his lips, his blond hair tousled, a lock of it falling across his forehead. Varakov thought the man looked as though he had himself sewed into his uniform each morning.

"You did not think, perhaps, to search for me in my

office? Or is that not covered in the KGB training school?"

Rozhdestvenskiy smiled, still standing more or less at attention, saying, "Comrade General—you are as noted for your wit as you are for your brilliant stratagems."

"That was not an answer to my question," Varakov said flatly, then turned to study the figures of the mastodons. "You have come to replace Karamatsov as head of the American branch of KGB. And you have come to tell me where the military and the KGB will draw the proverbial line. That is correct?"

He heard the voice behind him. "Yes, Comrade General—that is correct. The Politburo has decided—"

"I know what the Politburo has decided," Varakov told him evenly. "That the KGB should have greater authority here, and that you, as Karamatsov's best friend in life should be his successor in death. That KGB will have the final word—not the military."

"That is correct, Comrade General."

Varakov turned around, slowly, facing the vastly younger and slightly taller man.

Rozhdestvenskiy continued speaking. "In matters that strictly involve the military, of course, yours will be the final word, Comrade General. But in matters where the KGB—"

"In any matters," Varakov interrupted, "I am sure there will be KGB involvement, will there not?"

"So many incidents have unforeseen political ramifications, Comrade General—it may be difficult to avoid. May I smoke?"

"Yes—you may burn if you wish." Varakov nodded, half-wishing the man would. He watched as Rozhdestvenskiy took from under his uniform tunic a silver cigarette

34

case, the cigarettes in it looking more American than Russian; then a lighter that perfectly matched the case, and lit the cigarette in its steady flame. The new KGB colonel—the new Karamatsov, Varakov thought—like the man he replaced, was too reminiscent of a Nazi for Varakov to feel remotely comfortable around him. SS—the perfect physical specimen, the blond-haired superman—only this one was a Marxist rather than a National Socialist. "And what is your first order of business, Colonel?"

"Two matters are pressing, Comrade General. Perhaps not of the greatest importance, but something which must be accomplished. We do not know."

"I thought the KGB knew everything." Varakov smiled, starting to walk around the figures of the mastodons, still inspecting them as if they were his troops.

Rozhdestvenskiy smiled when Varakov glanced at him. "Hardly, Comrade General—but to know everything is our goal. No—this is a rather esoteric matter, perhaps; one with which you are conversant, I am sure. It is the matter of the mysterious Eden Project and what it actually was or is. Shortly before leaving our headquarters in Moscow, I learned of the efforts of a heroic Soviet agent. He had stolen some information regarding the Eden Project and information regarding other matters as well, things which were held at the highest security levels in what was the United States. Because of the sensitive nature of the information, he was bringing it to Moscow personally. When the war broke out—"

"Yes—do you recall? I believe it was Napoleon, wasn't it? A messenger reportedly came to him. Napoleon read the message and proclaimed something to the effect: 'My God, peace has broken out!' It was something like that."

"Yes, something like that, Comrade General." Rozhdestvenskiy nodded.

"This agent—what word did he bring you?" Varakov felt himself smile. "Surely not that peace had broken out."

"He brought word of precisely where duplicate files on the Eden Project were hidden, in addition to the first copy files which were destroyed during the bombing of the Johnson Space Center in Texas. There is now renewed hope that—"

"You hope for that then. I have more pressing matters than some American defense project so obscure that—"

"I know what you hope." Rozhdestvenskiy nodded. "As the wife of my lifelong friend Colonel Karamatsov, the life of Major Tiemerovna is my concern as well. Surely in all the troop movements from the East Coast of the continent there has been some word—"

"Nothing," Varakov answered sincerely. "She was last seen helping in the evacuation of Florida at an airfield, only moments before the major earthquake struck and a high-altitude observation plane photographed the beginning of the Florida peninsula's collapse into the ocean."

"She was with the American agent, Rourke, was she not, Comrade General?" Rozhdestvenskiy asked. Is he trying to sound innocent, Varakov asked himself, realizing that for an instant the charming, handsome, blond officer had penetrated his defenses, made him feel there was something of a genuine concern for Natalia's welfare.

"I believe so—but that is only from a—" he began defensively.

Rozhdestvenskiy cut him off. "A reliable report, I

believe, Comrade General? This other matter to which I hope to attend—I confess both a personal and professional interest in the safe return of your niece. The major may be able to aid me in locating the war criminal Rourke—"

"War criminal?" Varakov repeated, without really thinking.

"Surely, the assassination of the head of the American KGB by this Rourke is a war crime, Comrade General. I understand he was a physician before going into the employ of the American Central Intelligence Agency."

Varakov picked his words—carefully—for the first time realizing what kind of man he truly dealt with. "It is my understanding that this Dr. Rourke had left the CIA sometime before the war. I do not really concern myself with him. I belive his major preoccupation is searching for his wife and children who may have survived the war; I do not know. If you capture him, I should be interested in meeting him. But that is your affair."

"Yes, Comrade General. That is my affair." Rozhdestvenskiy dropped his cigarette to the marble floor and started to grind it out beneath the heel of his boot.

"But this is my headquarters building, Colonel; pick up that cigarette."

"But surely, a prisoner used for janitorial service can—"

"That is not the point; pick it up."

The boyish smile was gone from Rozhdestvenskiy's face. He hesitated a moment, then stooped over and picked up the cigarette butt, holding it between two manicured fingernails. "Will there be anything else, Comrade General?"

"No—I think not." Varakov turned and started back

across the main hall toward his office without walls.

Thousands of troops were moving inland to escape the raging storm fronts assaulting the eastern coast of what had been the United States—regrouping and searching, he hoped. That Natalia would be safe as long as she was with John Rourke, Varakov took as a fact. It was after that—with this Rozhdestvenskiy—that Varakov worried about her safety.

"Catherine!" He called out the name before he remembered he had told her to go and rest. He shrugged, deciding he would do the same thing himself. There might not be time for it in the future.

His hands stabbed into his pockets as he walked away from his office and he stopped once, glancing back over his right shoulder. The offensive SS-like KGB officer was gone from view. Varakov smiled, remembering the ego satisfaction he had given himself in making Rozhdestvenskiy pick up the cigarette. He realized as he glanced once more at the mastodons that he would likely pay for it, too, and perhaps so would Natalia.

Chapter 5

Rourke's knuckles were white, his fists bunched on the yoke now as the twin-engine cargo plane skimmed low over over the icy roadway, his starboard engine hopelessly iced. His mind went back to the only other time in his life he had crash-landed a plane—the 747 in the New Mexico desert on the Night of the War. He remembered Mrs. Richards, her husband gone in the destruction of the West Coast, her compassion in caring for the dying captain, her tireless help that long night while they had fought to keep airborne—then her death when the 747 had—Rourke wrenched back on the controls, trying to keep the nose up. The brakes held, but the plane started to skid as it hit the ice- and snow-covered road. "Get your heads down!" Rourke shouted to Paul, strapped in near the midsection, and to Natalia in the copilot's seat beside him.

"John!"

Rourke didn't look at her; he was feeling the tendons in his neck distending, his body suddenly cold, the air temperature finally getting to him. The plane was going out of control. He worked the flaps to decelerate, the brakes starting to slow him as well now. The straightaway stretched for perhaps another quarter-mile yet and if he slowed the craft too quickly the skid would become uncontrollable. The aircraft zigzagged under him, the tail of the craft whipping back and forth across the three-lane width of Kentucky highway. The straightaway was rapidly running out. Eyes squinted against the glare of the plane's lights on the snow, he could see ahead of him where the road seem to end, to curve in a sharp S-bend, running to his left. The plane coasted right across the icy road, toward the drop-off on the far end of the S-bend, a meager metal guardrail there and beyond it, from what Rourke could see, a drop.

Two hundred yards, perhaps less. Rourke controlled the plane with the flaps, the braking action worsening the skid. Rourke reached across to Natalia, punching the release button on the seat harness, grabbing her by the left shoulder, shouting back along the fuselage, "Paul— we're bailing out—get the cargo door and jump for it— jump as far out as you can!"

Rourke didn't wait to see that the younger man was complying, but grabbed Natalia, shoving her roughly ahead of him toward the fuselage door.

"John!" Rourke glanced to his left. Rubenstein was struggling with the seat belt, its buckling mechanism apparently jammed. "Save yourselves!"

Rourke glanced toward Natalia; the Russian woman was already working the handle on the cargo door with her left hand, in her right hand something metallic gleamed—a knife. She reached the butt of it out to Rourke. Rourke snatched it from her hand, wheeling, the aircraft's lurching and bumping throwing him toward Rubenstein. Collapsing against the fuselage, Rourke reached the knife blade under the webbing strap across

Paul's left shoulder, sliced it; then, as he started for the leg strap, he could feel the rush of arctic-feeling air, hear the slipstream. The fuselage door opened. Rourke's borrowed knife slashed apart the last of the restraints.

The knife still in his right hand, he snatched at his CAR-15, yelling to Paul, "Jump for it, Paul—go on!"

As Rourke was moving toward the door, the younger man was already on his feet, the Schmeisser in his right hand; Natalia was starting to jump. Rourke, at the fuselage door, wheeled, reaching toward his strapped-down Harley, cast a glance at it because it would likely be the last, and snatched his leather jacket. He turned and dove, the snow slamming up toward him as he rolled onto the road surface, his left shoulder taking it, aching as he hit, the rear stabilizers sawing through the air toward him as he flattened himself, the tail of the fuselage passing inches over his head.

He followed it with his eyes for an instant, then pushed himself to his feet, slipping on the ice, running, lurching forward. He could see Natalia, lying in the middle of the road, Paul running toward her. Rourke heard it, the wrenching and groaning of metal. He wheeled, skidding on the heels of his black combat boots across the ice, to watch as the plane crashed through the metal roadside barricade and disappeared over the side. He waited— there was no explosion. But there wasn't much hope either, he thought. Three people, one jacket, a rifle with no spare magazines and a submachine gun with no spare magazines. A few pistols. He looked into his hand—and a Bali-Song knife. He turned, starting back toward Natalia.

But like a little girl after taking a spill on an ice rink, she sat, legs wide apart, her right hand propping her up, her left hand brushing the hair back from her face, hair already flecked with snow. Beside her Rubenstein crouched, as if waiting.

Rourke stopped walking, a yard or so from her still. He held up the knife. "Never told me about the Bali-Song knife."

She only smiled. Rourke glanced back where the plane had disappeared; if anything could be salvaged, it would have to wait. The leather jacket was bunched in his left hand along with the CAR-15. He approached Natalia, squatted down beside her, and draped the coat across her shoulders. She was already shivering, as was Paul Rubenstein. And so was Rourke. . . .

"I had the Bali-Song for a long time. For some reason I didn't carry it when you found me in the desert. I don't remember why. But I took it with me to Florida, just in case."

"Are you good with it?" Rourke asked her, shivering.

"Yes. If my hands weren't so cold—I could show—" She shook from the freezing air temperature; subfreezing, perhaps close to zero, Rourke thought as he started down the side of the embankment, carefully, slowly, for the rocks that formed the purchases for his hands and feet were ice-coated. "Be careful, John."

"Once I get down there, I can snake up a rope; then you and Paul can join me and at least we'll have some shelter—unless it looks like it's going to blow or something."

"I can—" Rubenstein began.

"You stay with Natalia. If I break every bone in my body doing this, I want someone in one piece to take care of her." It was getting dark as Rourke started climbing again, the aircraft still some thirty feet below him, its portside wing broken in two, the starboard engine snagged in a clump of rocks some fifty feet farther below it and half-obscured now by snow.

Rourke's hands were numb as his fingers played along the glistening iced-over rocks, his shoulder still ached from where he'd hit the road surface, and one desire suddenly obsessed him—to urinate. Rourke's right foot edged down, then his left. The left slipped as loose shale under him, crusted over with ice, broke away from the dirt that had held it. His fingertips dug into the rock surface against which they pressed as his right foot braced against the coated rock against which only the toes now pressed.

"John—I'm coming down," Natalia shouted.

"No—I'll be—" Rourke swung his left leg out, finding a purchase against a gnarled stump of bush growing out of the dirt embankment. "I'm all right."

Rourke edged his right hand down onto a lower ledge of rock, then his left foot, then his left hand, then his right foot. Slowly, methodically, his kidneys screaming at him to let go, he kept moving.

His hands were numbed to the point where he could barely sense the rocks under his fingertips, and his feet were becoming chilled as well. A numbness was setting into his thighs. But the plane was nearer.

He glanced up once; Natalia and Paul, peered down at him, over the edge. The thought crossed his mind that even if one of the bikes had remained serviceable, how would they ever get it up to the road surface? And the freak storm—when would it end?

The plane was a few yards away from him now, across a wide break in the ground and below the break, a drop of seventy-five feet or more. Rourke settled himself against the rocks, checking his footing, then awkwardly because

43

of the narrowness of the ledge, swung his left leg around behind him, found a purchase for the left foot, then simultaneously swung his left arm out and around, twisting his body. He moved his feet slightly, firming the position he had, his back now against the rocks and dirt of the embankment. The snow, falling in larger, heavier flakes, covered his shoulders, lingered on his eyelashes—freezing him.

The jump to the opposite side of the break in the ground was only ten or eleven feet. But there was no running room. He would simply hurtle his body off the ledge and that would be it.

He sucked in his breath hard, glancing up one more time; he couldn't see either Natalia or Paul clearly because of the heaviness of the snowfall. "Now!" he rasped, pushing himself away from the embankment with his hands. His knees slightly flexed as he half-jumped, half-fell forward, his fingers reaching out. His right hand, then his left touched the opposite side of the open space, his hands clawing at the dirt and loose rocks there. His hands slipped, his thighs slamming down hard against the surface of the ground, his body starting back down the incline, slipping. He couldn't dig in his heels—his feet dangled in the air. As he started to slide backward, he spread-eagled his arms, his fingers clawing for a purchase on the ice-coated ground. A rock—he held it, then the rock dislodged and he was slipping again.

His left hand snaked behind him, snatching for the A.G. Russell Black Chrome Sting IA he carried in the little inside waistband holster. His fingers closed stiffly around it as he slipped toward the edge, his left arm swinging around his body in a wide arc. The point of the Sting IA bit deep into the ground, penetrating the ice. His right hand grasped for the knife handle as well now, both fists bunched around it; his body below the breastbone dangled in midair.

He sucked in his breath, flexing his arm muscles as he tried pulling himself up. There wasn't time; the knife was already slipping from the soft dirt beneath the ice, and his cold-numbed fingers were slipping from the slick steel of the knife's handle.

"No!" Rourke heard the shout come from his lips and for the first time became conscious of it. Summoning all his strength, he drew himself up. The knife slipped from the dirt; his body lurched forward, onto the ice and snow. He rolled, flattening himself, the knife still clutched in his left fist.

He couldn't see through the snow now to the road thirty feet above, but through the whiteness he heard a voice. "Answer me, John—John!" It was Natalia.

"I'm all right," Rourke shouted back, already starting to edge across the ice.

Two yards from the still intact fuselage, he stood up, slowly edging forward. He started into the plane, but stopped.

His stiff right thumb and first finger worked at his zipper; there was something more important than inspecting the plane that instant. . . .

He stood inside, shivering with the cold, but at least out of the wind. Natalia's borrowed motorcycle, a vintage BSA, had been the first of the three, farthest forward in the fuselage; the other two bikes had hammered against it in the crash. It was twisted, as was the underside of the fuselage where apparently the craft had gouged against a large rock, or one of the supports for the steel guardrail.

45

But his own jet black Harley-Davidson Low Rider appeared undamaged, as was the bright blue Low Rider he had found for Paul Rubenstein after the younger man's motorcycle had been abandoned to lighten the plane during the Florida evacuation.

With effort, still shivering, he got Rubenstein's bike aside so he could get to his own. The Lowe Alpine Systems Loco Pack was still strapped in place behind the seat. Rourke got to it, opening one of the pockets. There was a red-and-silver Thermos Space Blanket, the kind larger than the original disposable models developed for the astronaut program. The silver reflective side toward him, he wrapped the blanket around his shoulders, leaning heavily against one of the fuselage ribs. Rourke rammed his hands, palms inward, down inside the front of his trousers, warming them against his testicles to reduce the numbness of his fingers so he could move them well enough to work. He stood there, the blanket around him, his hands starting to get back feeling, his eyes flickering from one part of the fuselage to another—the damage.

The plane was a total loss, as he had realized it would be from the first moment he had decided to abandon it, when stopping it on the ice-slicked road surface had proven impossible. It would have been unlikely that the iced and stalled engine could have been successfully repaired in any event. It had been the single-engine landing that had caused the problem with stopping in the first place—not enough power. Aside from Natalia's motorcycle, everything that was important seemed relatively unscathed.

He could move his fingers more now, so he withdrew his hands from inside his pants, then quickly started going through his things and the packs of Natalia and of Paul Rubenstein. . . .

A pair of vintage, heavy leather Kombi ski gloves on his hands, a seen-better-days gray woolen crew-neck sweater on over his shirt, Rourke fed out part of the climbing rope from his pack, a rock secured to the free end. "Stand back from the edge up there—got a chunk of rock on the end of this for weight."

"Understand," Paul Rubenstein's voice called back through the snow. Rourke still could not see sufficiently well through the heavily falling snow to view the road surface above him. He started swinging the free end of the rope, the end weighted with the rock, feeding out more and more of the line. He made the toss, then heard the sound of the rock slamming against something metallic—one of the supports for the guardrail? The rope slacked and he started reeling it back in. He would have to try again. . . .

On the fourth try, the weighted end of the rope didn't move. "Paul—look for it!"

For a moment, there was no answer, then Rubenstein's voice responded, "I've got it, John."

Rourke nodded to himself, then shouted, "Secure it to something really sturdy—have Natalia help you!" He waited then. Telling Paul to get Natalia's help was the tactful way of handling the fact that Rourke had no idea how well or how poorly the younger man could tie knots. And Rourke very well understood the sort of training Natalia had undergone to become a KGB field agent in the first place—rappelling would have been part of it and she'd make the knot secure if Rubenstein didn't.

"It's set, John," Natalia's voice called down.

47

"Haul up on the rope—hurry up," Rourke called up. On the near end of the rope, Rourke had Natalia's and Paul's winter jackets secured. The rope started snaking upward. . . .

As Rourke huddled by the fire a few yards from the aircraft fuselage, the water nearly boiling, he considered Rubenstein; the younger man had made it down the embankment quite well. Not as professionally as Natalia had let herself down, but well nonetheless.

The water in the pot was boiling and Rourke picked it up by the handle, his left hand still gloved and insulating his fingers; then he stood up. He hated to, but he had to—he kicked out the fire. The darkness around him was more real now as he started toward the glowing light of the Coleman lamp in the fuselage.

The Space Blanket was wrapped around Natalia now, her coat being rather light for the extreme cold of the night. Rourke was chilled still, despite the fact that he had added the leather bomber-style jacket over his sweater. Rubenstein looked positively frozen to the bone, Rourke thought.

"Paul—why don't you fish through the gear and find a bottle of whiskey? I think we could all use a drink." Rourke smiled, watching Rubenstein's face almost instantly brighten. The younger man was up and moving as Rourke crouched down beside Natalia near the Coleman lamp.

"Here—I'll do that," she said, her gloved hands reaching for the pot of no-longer-boiling water. "You hold the food packets."

"All right," Rourke murmured. There wasn't much of the Mountain House food left in his gear and he'd have to

48

resupply once he got back to the Retreat, he reminded himself.

"Hope you like beef stroganoff," Rourke said, holding the first of the opened packets up for her to add the water.

"Do you remember the camp we had that night before you scouted for the Brigands and the Paramils—in Texas?"

"Yes," Rourke told her.

"Should I get drunk again?" She smiled. "But it wouldn't do me any good, would it?"

Rourke, balancing one of the Mountain House packs, then opening another, said nothing. He turned to call to Rubenstein, still searching for the bottle. "Food's on, Paul."

"John," Natalia's alto insisted. "You remember that? I called you Mr. Goodie-Goodie, didn't I."

"It doesn't matter," Rourke told her, his voice a whisper.

"I think I loved you then, too," she said matter-of-factly.

Rourke looked into her eyes a moment. "I think I loved you then, too."

"I won't see you after we get out of here, after this storm—will I?"

Rourke didn't answer.

Rubenstein came up, an unopened quart bottle of Seagram's Seven in his hands. "This bottle's cold—least we won't need any ice, huh?" The younger man laughed.

"Here, Paul." Natalia handed Rubenstein the first of the three packs, the one with the hottest water added. Rourke exchanged a glance with her and she smiled.

Rubenstein took the pack of beef stroganoff and settled himself beside the Coleman lamp. "Like old times—out there on the desert in Texas," Rubenstein remarked, giving the food a final stir.

"John and I were just saying that," Natalia told him.

"This is good." Rubenstein's garbled voice came back through a mouthful of food.

Rourke broke the seal on the whiskey bottle, twisting open the cap and handing the bottle to Natalia. "I'll get a cup for you," he started.

"No—like we did that other time." She smiled, putting the bottle to her lips and tilting her head back to let the liquid flow through the bottle's neck and into her mouth. Rourke watched her, intently.

She handed him the bottle and, not wiping it, he touched the mouth of the bottle to his lips, taking a long swallow; then, as he passed the bottle to Rubenstein, he said to her—Natalia—"Like we did the other time."

He glanced at Rubenstein for a moment, but the younger man, having already set the bottle down, was smiling and saying, "Not like I did the other time. I can still remember the headache." And he continued with his food. . . .

Natalia lay in Rourke's arms, the Coleman lamp extinguished. Rubenstein was taking a turn at watch just inside the open cargo hatch of the fuselage. "You'll pick up the search for Sarah and the children? I'd help if I could."

"I don't suppose it matters; an intelligence operative of Reed's in Savannah, retired Army guy, reactivated for this—"

"The Resistance? I wonder if it has a prayer," she mused.

"I don't think that's the point of it anyway," Rourke whispered to her in the darkness. "It's the doing that matters, the results are secondary. But he got word to Reed at U.S. II headquarters that he'd made a positive identification of Sarah and Michael and Annie—they were heading toward U.S. II headquarters."

"But—"

Rourke cut her off. "U.S. II headquarters was moving out so your people wouldn't make a raid and catch Chambers. And Sarah and the children couldn't make it across the Mississippi valley anyway—the radiation. So I've gotta stop them—before they get into the fallout zone."

"If somehow we learn anything in Chicago, I will or my uncle will—we'll get word to you, somehow."

"I know that," Rourke answered.

"I hope you find them, John—and that they are well, and whole, and that you can make a life for them. Somewhere."

"The Retreat," Rourke said emotionlessly. "The Retreat—only place safe. It's safe against anything except a direct hit, enough supplies to live for years, growing lights for the plants to replenish the oxygen—and that stream gives me electrical power. I can seal the place to make it airtight. But Sarah was right in a way; it *is* a cave. I don't know if I can see raising two children in a cave—even a cave with all the conveniences."

"You don't have any choice—you didn't start the war," she said, her voice suddenly guilt-tinged he thought.

"Neither did you, Natalia—neither did you," he murmured. She leaned tighter against him and he held her tighter.

"If I close my eyes, I can imagine it."

"What?" he asked, feeling dumb for saying it.

"That things were different and we could be—" She didn't finish the thought.

Rourke touched his lips to her forehead as he leaned back, her head on his shoulder. As he closed his eyes, he murmured the word that she hadn't said—"lovers." He listened to the evenness of her breathing long past the time he should have fallen asleep. . . .

Using the rope—all of it—Rourke and Natalia had engineered a pulley system for getting the bikes up onto the highway. And he was committed now, he knew. The storm showed no signs of abating, but the longer he delayed taking up the search, the closer Sarah and the children might get to the irradiated zone, the more chance there was that they would slip through his fingers. He wanted to catch up with them in the Carolinas—it was the only chance now.

It was the only chance now, because without the plane, it would be impossible to drop Natalia safely near Russian-dominated territory—northern Indiana. Rourke's original plan had been to leave Natalia where she would be safe, then to drop Paul in Tennessee. He would have flown then as close to Savannah as possible—he and Paul catching Sarah and the children between them.

The very act of starting one motorcycle toward the road was a commitment to abandon the shelter of the aircraft fuselage, for one man by himself could not control the bike and get the bike elevated—even with Natalia helping him. And now, as Rourke coiled the last of the ropes, his own Harley and Paul's bike as well on the road surface, he glanced back down to the shelter of the fuselage. He was already chilled, despite the fact that he wore two pairs of jeans, three shirts, his crew-necked

52

sweater, and jacket. Using spare bootlaces, he had secured Natalia's sleeping bag over her coat, to give her added warmth. She would ride behind Paul on his bike.

The plan was simple—the only one possible under the circumstances. The heart of the storm seemed to be to the south and west. With luck, Paul and Natalia would be driving out of the storm while he, Rourke, drove into it. With its intensity, Rourke assumed it couldn't last much longer at any event.

Rourke would start from Tennessee and cut down into Georgia, perhaps as far down as the massive craters that had once been metropolitan Atlanta; he still had a Geiger counter, as did Paul. Then he would zigzag back and forth with his farthest range being the lower Carolinas. Paul, after leaving Natalia in safe territory, would travel back, retracing the route down from northern Indiana to Tennessee, then strike straight for Savannah from there. With luck one of them would intercept Sarah and Michael and Annie. In two weeks, he and Paul would rendezvous at the Retreat—hopefully one of them with Rourke's family in tow.

The Metalifed and Mag-Na-Ported six-inch Colt Python in the flap holster at his waist, Rourke began making a last minute check of his gear. The Python and his other guns had been freshly lubricated with Break-Free CLP which would resist the sub-freezing temperatures. The Lowe Alpine Systems Loco pack was secure behind the seat of the Low Rider, the CAR-15 wrapped in plastic and secured to the pack, a blanket under the plastic to protect the gun in the event of a skid. He glanced along the icy road surface; a skid was highly likely.

He started his bike, letting the engine warm up as he walked back toward Natalia and Paul. Rubenstein's bike was already loaded and started.

Rubenstein started to say something, but Rourke cut him off. He wasn't certain why, but an urgency seemed now to obsess him. "You memorized those strategic fuel supply locations so you can get gasoline?"

"Yes—yeah, I did," the younger man said, looking strange without his glasses; but with the snow falling, it would have been impossible to see through them.

"And take it real slow—really slow until you start getting out of this. Just be careful all the way, even after you've gotten through the weather—a sudden temperature—"

"John—I'll do all right. Take it easy." Rubenstein extended his gloved right hand, then pulled the glove away.

Rourke hesitated a moment, then pulled off his own glove. "I know you will Paul—I know. I just—ahh . . ." Rourke simply shook his head, clamping his jaw tight and wishing he had a cigar there to chew on.

"I'll walk you back to your motorcycle," Natalia said quietly, taking Rourke's bare right hand as soon as he released Paul's grip.

"All right," Rourke answered her softly. "I'll see you Paul."

"Yeah, John. I'll be right behind you real soon."

Rourke simply nodded, then started back toward his machine, feeling the pressure of Natalia's hand inside his. Her hand was warm. He looked at her once, then looked away. One of his big bandanna handkerchiefs was tied over her head to cover her ears; his own ears were freezing. It was blue, making the blueness of her eyes even bluer. The sleeping bag bound around her made her figure virtually vanish under it and finally, as they stopped beside his Harley, without looking at her he murmured, "If you ever need to disguise yourself as a plump Russian peasant girl that's the perfect outfit."

He felt her hand let go of his, then her hand on his face as he turned to her.

"I love you, John Rourke—I'll always love you. Forever." She kissed his mouth hard, and he thought he saw a faint trace of a smile—a strained smile—on her face. She turned and ran away, almost slipping once on the ice as he watched her. She clambered aboard the snow-splotched bright blue Harley Low Rider and didn't look back as Rubenstein gunned the machine, shot a wave over his shoulder, and started off.

John Rourke stood there for a moment—cold. He was alone. It was a lifelong habit.

Chapter 6

Natalia Anastasia Tiemerovna hugged her arms tightly around Paul Rubenstein; she thought of him as a brother, as Rourke thought of him. Rourke had said it to her more than once. She held Paul in order to stay aboard the slowly moving motorcycle, and for the warmth his body radiated—and to give him the warmth of her body.

It had been three hours by the face of her ladies' Rolex and the ice and snow had allowed them, she estimated, not more than a hundred miles, perhaps less. "Do you think the storm will intensify as John heads south?" she asked.

There was no answer from Rubenstein. She repeated the question—louder. "Do you think the storm will intensify—as John goes south, Paul?"

"I think so. Maybe slacking up a little soon for us— looks like it up—"

"Paul!" It was the first time he'd turned his face toward her in more than an hour. His eyebrows were crusted over with ice, his face red and raw to the point of bleeding on his cheeks. She suddenly realized that while his body had shielded hers from the wind, his face had had nothing to protect it. "Stop the bike—now. You have to," she shouted to him.

"What—" But then he shook his head slowly and she could hear the sounds of engine compression as he geared down, making the stop slowly to avoid a skid. They had almost had one perhaps ten miles back but Rubenstein had kept the bike aright somehow, although Natalia didn't know how he had done it.

The bike slowed then, stopping, slipping a little as Paul shifted his weight, Natalia's feet going out to balance it as well. "You let me drive," she said, dismounting.

Paul looked at her, his eyes tearing from the wind, but smiling despite it. "If I let anything happen to your face—well, aside from the fact John'd never forgive me—I wouldn't forgive myself," he told her.

She threw her arms around his neck, hugging him a moment, then stepped back.

She had long ago resigned herself to Rourke's chauvinism—and liked it in her heart. And Rubenstein treated her the same way. She pulled the blue-and-white bandanna from her hair, her ears instantly feeling the cold. She started toward Rubenstein again, saying, "Then you tie this over your face and stop for five minutes every half-hour—either that or I don't go another mile, Paul."

"But—"

"No!" She decided then that if Paul insisted on treating her like a woman, then she could treat him like a little boy—and impose her will. She bound the handkerchief at the back of his neck, pulling up the sides until the handkerchief covered all his face just below his eyes. "You look very, very much like a bandit—a handsome bandit." She smiled.

Rubenstein shook his head, shrugging his shoulders,

his voice sounding slightly muffled as he said, "We go again?"

"Yes—if you think you can. But only for a half-hour—then a rest."

"Agreed," Rubenstein told her, straddling the Harley once more. She climbed on behind him. As the machine started along the road, she huddled her head down into the sleeping bag which formed a collar for her—at least as much as she could, for her ears tingled already with the cold despite her hair covering them.

She had bathed his face and now massaged it as they huddled from the slightly diminished storm under the shelter of a bridge, ground clothes anchored to the bike and to the bridge itself to form a windbreak for them. It was dark—night had come early because of the darkness that had filled the skies throughout the day. "You don't have to—"

She cut him off. "I massage your face because I love you and want you to be well."

He turned and looked at her. "You don't have to—"

"I do. I love both of you. You know that."

"But you love him differently—I know that, too. The kid isn't always asleep when you think he is." Rubenstein smiled, then winced, his face evidently hurting when he moved.

"Rest," she told Paul.

"He's a funny guy, isn't he? John, I mean," Paul Rubenstein said, as if to himself, she thought.

"Yes—he is," she answered, wishing for a cigarette but still needing to rub his face to restore the circulation. "How are your feet and hands?"

"Left foot's a little stiff—but I don't think it's—"

"Rourke isn't the only one who knows about the damage cold can do to the body," she said reprovingly. "Lean back."

"Hey, no—I can—"

"Do as I say," Natalia told him. She started undoing the laces of his left boot, getting the boot free; it felt damp to her. Then she removed the two socks that covered his foot. The sole of his foot was yellow. "This could turn to frostbite—very quickly," she snapped. She opened the front of her coat, throwing back as well the sleeping bag that covered her. Reaching under her coat, under the shirt Rourke had given her, to the front of her black jump suit, she zipped it down, then took Rubenstein's foot and placed it against the bare flesh of her abdomen.

"Hey—you—"

"Let me! Tell me when the feeling starts back. How is the other foot?"

"It's well, it's okay."

"Keep your foot here and don't move it," she ordered, reaching down to his other foot and starting to work on the boot laces—her own fingers were numb, and her ears still felt the cold from the slipstream of the bike as they'd ridden.

"That bandanna you put over my face against the wind—it smelled like you. I guess from your hair," Rubenstein concluded, sounding lame.

"Thank you, Paul," Natalia whispered, getting the two socks off his right foot. The sole of his foot was yellow, but not as bad as the left one had been. Again, she felt the almost icy flesh against her abdomen and she shivered.

"You love John—I mean really love him, don't you?" Rubenstein blurted out.

She closed her eyes a moment, felt pressure there

59

against her eyelids, then opened them. "Yes—you know
I do."

"I'm sorry—I mean for both of you. John and Sarah—
I mean it's none of my business—"

"No—talk if you want," she told him.

"He—well, it's because he doesn't know if she's safe, if
she's alive minute by minute—that's—"

"I heard the lines in an American movie once—'I can't
fight a ghost'? No—even a living ghost. And I don't want
to fight it. I respect John for searching for Sarah. For—"
She almost said never touching her. But she couldn't say
that because she didn't like to think about it.

"I mean . . . he's the last of a breed, isn't he? Silent,
strong—a man of honor."

"Yes—he's a man of honor," she repeated. The chills
in her body from the coldness of Rubenstein's feet were
starting to subside. . . .

They had built a fire; there had been no other choice.
And behind the windbreak in the glow of the fire, her feet
wrapped in the sleeping bag and blankets around her,
even covering her head, her ears were finally starting to
become warmer.

Paul sat a foot or so away from her, the whiskey bottle
beside them, between them. He had taken a long drink
from it an hour earlier and then simply sat, watching the
fire, silent, his feet wrapped in blankets against the cold.

"She used to do that. I always had problems with my
feet freezing up," Paul said suddenly.

"Your—"

"My girl—I was afraid you were gonna say my mother.
But it was my girl."

"Was she—was she pretty?" Natalia asked, not
looking at him, but staring into the fire.

60

"Yeah—she was pretty. She was," he said with an air of finality.

Natalia felt suddenly awkward, reaching her hand out of the blankets which swathed her, the cold air something she could feel suddenly against her skin. She picked up the bottle—the glass of it was cold to her touch and cold against her lips as she drank from it, then set it down again. She reached her hand out still farther, found Rubenstein's arm and held it. "Would you tell me about her?"

"Catharsis?"

"Maybe—and my curiosity. You know that. Women are always curious."

"Ruth was that way," he said quietly.

"Had you—?"

"Known each other a long time? Yeah—went to temple together whenever my dad was on leave when we were kids. Her folks and my folks knew each other."

"You were a military brat weren't you?" Natalia smiled, looking at him in the firelight.

"Yeah—brat period, maybe. But that isn't true. I was always a good kid—relatives, the other officers, always said, 'Paul is such a well-behaved little boy.' Wish I hadn't been. Ruth always said we should wait until we—" He stopped and fell silent.

Natalia didn't know if she should press it, but then decided. "Until you were married?"

He just looked at her, his glasses, long since back in place, slipping down the bridge of his nose. "You believe that . . . I mean, well you know . . . but this isn't any kind of thing on my part to try to—"

"To make a pass?" Natalia smiled.

"Yeah—that'd be pretty funny—me making a pass for

61

you, wouldn't it?" He laughed.

"No—and it wouldn't even be sweet. But it'd be flattering to me." She smiled.

Again he fell silent, taking a pull on the bottle, then settling his forearm under her left hand again. "Here I am—middle of nowhere and I'm a virgin. Just what you want with death around every corner, isn't it?" He laughed.

"You would make any woman a fine lover," Natalia said, feeling awkward saying it.

"Hell! I knew Ruth for six years before I worked up the nerve to kiss her." Rubenstein laughed.

But the laughter sounded hollow to her, and Natalia said, "How old were you then?"

"Nine." He laughed again, this time the laughter sounded genuine she thought.

"I met Vladmir when I was twenty. He was so strong and brave and—I didn't know any better. He made love to me—a lot in those days. I thought it was love anyway."

She moved her hand away, finding the black shoulder bag and starting to search it for her cigarettes. She set her knife down on the ground beside the bag.

"What'd you call that knife again?" Rubenstein asked, obviously changing the subject. "What was it?"

"A Bali-Song knife—it's a Philippine design, though it may have originated with an American sailor who brought it there. Some of the really big ones were used as cane knives and as weapons, too. It's a martial-arts fighting knife. I got into martial-arts weapons when I was just—"

She put the knife down, looking at Paul. "Why don't you ask—did I ever really love Vladmir?"

She lit a cigarette, waiting for him to ask her.

"Did you?" he finally said, his voice sounding suddenly older to her.

"Yes—until I found out what he was. And I was trying to deal with that and I saw John again there and—" She swallowed hard, forgetting about the cigarette a moment, then choking on the smoke and coughing.

"John was everything you'd thought Vladimir was—but really wasn't. I mean, the grammar or syntax or whatever—well it really sucks, but isn't that what you want to say?"

Natalia swallowed again, this time without the smoke—instead the bottle in her left hand, the whiskey burning at her throat suddenly. "Yes—I wanted to say that. Men always jokingly say women are like children, call them girls—but we are. We all look for our own personal knight—you know, the kind with a 'K-N-I—' We look for someone we hook our dreams on. That's what Ruth saw in you—and she wasn't wrong."

"Me—a knight?" Rubenstein laughed.

"A knight doesn't have to be tall and brave—but you are brave, you just maybe didn't know it then. It's inside. That's what it is." She reached her hand out and felt Rubenstein's hand touching hers. "That's what it is," she repeated.

Chapter 7

Nehemiah Rozhdestvenskiy thought the idea was, in a way, amusing. He looked at his gun—a nickel-plated Colt single-action Army .45 with a four-and-three-quarter-inch barrel. He was the conqueror, the invader, and his sidearm was "The Gun That Won the West"—as American as—he verbalized it, "Apple pie—ha!"

He cocked the hammer back to the loading notch, opened the loading gate, and spun the cylinder—five rounds, originally round-nosed lead solids, but the bullets drilled out three sixty-fourths of an inch with a one-sixteenth-inch drill bit, then tipped into candle wax after first having had an infinitesimal amount of powdered glass shavings inserted into their cavities. His own special load.

After rotating the cylinder, closing the gate, and lowering the hammer over the empty chamber, he holstered the gun inside his waistband, in a small holster he'd had custom-made of alligator skin, the gun with ivory butt forward and slightly behind his left hip bone. He reached to the dresser top, picking up the set of military brushes and working his hair with them. Thirty-four years old and not a speck of gray, he thought.

He set down the brushes and walked across the room to his closet; the clothes were neatly arranged there by his valet. He took down a tweed sportcoat—woolen and finely tailored to his exact measurements. He held it for a moment against the charcoal gray slacks he wore. The herringbone pattern had a definite charcoal gray shading and it made for a perfect combination.

He slipped the coat on. It would be cold, dangerous because of the storm—but it was vital and no choice was left other than to go.

He tried to think if there was some American song about West Virginia—his destination. He thought for a moment, then decided there doubtless was but he didn't know it. Instead he whistled "Dixie"—it was close enough for his purposes.

He stopped whistling as he reached the door of his quarters, laughing.

"Whistling 'Dixie' in a snowstorm—ha!"

He started through the doorway, into the hall. . . .

The wind at the restored Lake Front airport was bitingly cold, and he pulled up on the collar of his coat—wolf's fur—as he started toward the helicopter for the first leg of his journey toward West Virginia and the presidential retreat—and the duplicate set of files on the American Eden Project.

As he crossed under the rotor blades, he could feel it—his hair was ruined.

Chapter 8

Darkness had fallen deeply—he glanced at the black luminous face of the Rolex Submariner he wore—more than an hour ago. Rourke exhaled, watching the steam on his breath. The Harley's engine rumbled between his legs, running a little roughly with the cold.

A smile crossed his lips; he had been right. He was heading into the heart of the storm, Natalia and Paul away from it. He looked behind him once, into the white swirling darkness, then gunned the Harley, slowly starting ahead, the snow making the road almost impassable. . . .

Rourke had stopped a little while earlier to pull up the neck of his crew-neck sweater so that it covered most of his face, and his ears and head. There had been a sudden coldness near the small of his back where his sweater no longer protected him, and his ears had been stiffening with the cold. Now as he pressed the bike along a mountain curve, the visibility was bad, worse than it had been before. The storm only seemed to intensify as he moved along, and the cold increased. He wore his dark-lensed aviator-style sunglasses, to protect his eyes from the driving ice spicules; the backs of his gloved hands were encrusted with the ice where his fists locked over the handlebars. Brushing the ice away from the cuff of his sweater where it extended past his brown leather jacket's cuff, he moved his right hand to roll back the sweater and read the face of his watch. It was early in the evening, and the temperature would still drop for another nine or ten hours or so until just before dawn. As he shifted his right hand back to the handlebars, his weight shifted— stiffness from the cold—and the bike started into a skid.

He was doing barely twenty by the speedometer, the headlight of the Harley dancing wildly across the snow and ice as he took the curve, the Harley almost out of control. His hands wrestled the controls, trying to steer the bike out of the skid. His feet dragged to stop it, to balance it.

He let the bike skid out, jumping clear of it, the machine sliding across the road surface as he rolled. The Harley stopped in a snowbank to the far right of the road; Rourke landed flat on his stomach on the ice and snow.

He looked up, shaking his head to clear it.

He pushed himself up with his hands, slowly rising to his feet, pulling off his right glove, clutching the wrist hole tight in his left fist to retain the warmth inside. Then, with his right hand, he took off the glasses that had protected his eyes. He realized also that he was tired, fast approaching exhaustion; and with the cold, that could be fatal. He moved slowly, carefully toward his bike. It was in a snowbank, the snow having cushioned its impact. It appeared totally undamaged.

"Lucky," he murmured. He reached down and shut off the key, putting the glasses into an inside pocket of the jacket first. Squinting against the ice, he looked around him; he needed shelter. To his left—to the east—the clouds had a strange glow. Radiation? He shook his head, dismissing the thought. He could be dying at this very instant, he realized, if the snow that fell on him was irradiated. He would worry about that later.

But there was a subtle glow and trails of fire were visible; and as the cloud patterns shifted in the wind, the glow remained, as if it emanated from the ground.

If things had been normal, he would have labeled the glow as the lights from—he verbalized it—"A town—a town. A town." It looked to be about two or three miles away, but he realized that with the darkness and the snow and the cloud layers the distance judgment he made could have been self-deceptive.

He gloved his right hand again, working his fingers which were already stiffening..

There were two possibilities: to fabricate a shelter which would give marginal protection from the wind and no protection from the cold, or to go to the source of the lights. He had passed a side road turnoff a half-mile back; it likely led toward the source of the lights. The general direction seemed the same, although mountain roads, winding like Christmas ribbons across the landscape and really leading nowhere, could be deceptive as to direction. But along such a road there would be farms, homes—he decided.

His best chance for shelter was along the side road, though the snow would be heavier there.

He wrestled the Harley up, straddling it, starting it, the engine rumbling; his gas gauge was low, very low. Rourke fought the machine back out of the snowdrift and arced it around. If he kept the speed low enough . . .

Chapter 9

When more Brigands had started arriving—some sort of conclave she wondered?—she had awakened the children; then as silently as possible, she led them and the horses down on the far side of the rise—away from the Brigand camp, into the mounting storm. As Sarah rode Tildie now, the horse's body white-coated with the snow and ice, she wondered if it had been a wise decision—the right one? What would John have done? Would he have—?

"Mommie?"

She shook her head, smiling as she turned around. "What is it, Annie? Are you cold?"

"No—I'm letting her hug me—she isn't—"

"I *am* cold," Annie interrupted Michael. "I'm cold. I'm cold."

"Slow up, Michael," Sarah told her son, wanting him to rein in Sam. Michael didn't argue; she guessed he was cold, too. "Here." She reined Tildie around, then came up beside her children. She took the blanket which she had wrapped around her and put it around Annie's shoulders, wrapping her and Michael in it, pinning the blanket with her shaking hands across Michael's chest.

"But now you're gonna be cold, Mom," Michael protested.

"No. I won't lie and say I was too warm before, but I'll be fine. That should be better now," she said, turning to Annie. She stuffed her hands back into her gloves. She knew it wouldn't really be better; blankets only served to retain body warmth, not promote it, and both of the children were rapidly losing theirs. Again she wished for John to be there. He was a doctor, and among other things an expert on cold-weather survival.

She urged Tildie forward, telling Michael, "Stay here a minute. I'm going up that rise to see where we are—maybe."

"We can come," Michael insisted.

"All right—but stay well behind me—no sense wearing out Sam more than you have to."

She rode toward a tall stand of pines, the modified AR-15 across her saddle, cold against her thighs. If a Brigand conclave was on, then there would be Brigands traveling through the area, toward it.

Urging Tildie up the rise with her knees, her left hand holding the reins, she clutched the AR-15 pistol grip in her gloved right fist. "Come on, Tildie—just a little while longer," she cooed. Sarah glanced behind her once—Michael and Annie were coming, slowly, as she wanted them to. Michael, like his father, stubborn, arrogant, but reliable—a man she could count on more than he knew.

She was tempted to call out to the children, telling Michael to save Sam the haul up the rise, but she didn't, lest there be Brigands nearby she couldn't see.

Her eyelashes were encrusted with ice, the sleet and snow blowing against her face. She reached the top of the rise, reining Tildie back. "Whoa—easy," she cooed again.

Beyond the rise was the Savannah River and suddenly, she knew where she was. Lake Hartwell would be nearby—in the distance, she could see the Hartwell dam. John had taken her there once with the children for a tour of the dam structure, and several times she had gone to the lake itself with John and the children—swimming.

The thought of plunging her body into water now chilled her. She trembled, then trembled again, remembering John's hands on her once as they'd lain by the lake, their bodies wet and mostly naked, the children splashing in the water at its edge.

She turned to call out to Michael that everything was all right. Tildie reared; Sarah was thrown back in the stock saddle, a gunshot punching into the snow by the animal's front hoofs.

Sarah glanced to her right. Out of the pines were coming men and women, ragged, running, snow-covered, rifles and handguns in their hands, curses coming from their lips—and threats.

"Shit!" she screamed, wheeling Tildie, fighting to control the animal, and swinging the rifle up as she reined the horse under her. Her stiff-with-the-cold right thumb worked the selector to full auto position; her first finger twitched against the trigger. A short burst fired across her saddle; flowers of red blotched the ice-encrusted chest of the lead man. The man lunged toward her and the horse, an ax in his hands. They weren't Brigands; they were starving men and women, people who—she fired again, at another man starting to fire a shotgun. Sarah shot him in the face and neck, then

71

screamed, "Michael—get Sam going. Get Annie out of here!"

Sarah dug her heels into the frightened horse she rode; Tildie leaped ahead, back down the rise. A woman was lunging for her, out of the trees, a knife in bony hands held like a stake that was to be driven into someone's heart. Sarah pumped the AR-15's trigger again. The woman's body rocked back, spinning, then falling, a ragged line of red across the threadbare clothes covering her body.

She knew what they wanted now—the horse for food, the weapons for defense, her life and the children's lives. "Michael—get out of here," she shouted again, kneeing Tildie onward.

The pine boughs to her left shuddered, and in the darkness against the whiteness of the snow, she could see a man coming out of the trees, running toward her. She recognized what he had in his right hand—a machete.

He threw himself toward Tildie, into the animal's path. Tildie rearing under her, Sarah reined up, as the machete sliced toward Tildie's neck. The reins came away in Sarah's hands. She reeled back as the man sliced his blade again. Her left hand, still clutching at the useless reins, reached downward, snatching at Tildie's bridle. Sarah kneed the animal. "Come on, girl!"

Tildie leaped forward. The man hacked with his machete, but fell aside at the impact of the animal. Then he was on his feet and running after her as Sarah glanced back. She loosed the bridle, snatching at a generous handful of flowing ice-encrusted mane, and digging her heels into the bay mare's sides, coaching her. "Up, Tildie—up, girl." The animal responded, charging ahead and down the rise.

Ahead of her now, she could see Michael's horse, Michael and Annie aboard it. The thought suddenly startled her—Michael's horse. It was John's horse. Two figures wrestled against the front of the animal, reaching for the reins. Michael edged the animal back from them. She saw something flash against the snow, heard a scream; Michael had a knife. Where had he gotten it?

One of the two figures fell away, the second dove toward the two children in the saddle.

Sarah hauled back on Tildie's mane, the animal slowing, skidding along the snow on its haunches. Sarah's right hand brought the rifle up to her shoulder, her finger reached for the trigger. "Help my aim, God," she breathed, twitching the trigger as Tildie settled; the man, reaching for Michael and Annie, spun, fell.

"Get going, Michael!" Sarah screamed. Sam spurred ahead as she saw Michael kicking at him with his heels. Sarah dug in her knees, and Tildie started after him.

There was a burst of gunfire from behind her now, and Tildie started to slip on a patch of ice beneath her. Sarah felt the animal going down, perhaps wounded; she threw herself free of the animal's bulk, into the snow. Her back ached as she impacted, the rifle skittering across the ice, back toward Tildie.

Sarah rolled onto her belly and screamed, "No!" She pushed herself up to her knees. The burly man with the machete who'd tried for her back in the pines was coming.

Sarah glanced toward Tildie; the mare was up, apparently unhurt. Sarah started to her feet, running toward her rifle, then for the horse. She slipped, falling

73

forward, the rifle still several feet from her. She rolled onto her side, fumbling under the shaggy woolen coat she wore, under her sweater and her T-shirt, for John's Government Model .45. She had it out, in her right hand, her right thumb cocking the hammer as the man with the machete shrieked and threw himself toward her.

Her first finger pumped the trigger. The .45 rocked in her right hand, and the massive body rolled toward her.

Her mind flashed—why did all the others look half-starved when this man was fat?

As his body rolled toward her, she knew why. Around his neck was a necklace; the teeth were human.

"You bastard!" she screamed as his head lolled toward her and he started pushing himself off the ice, the left hand, blood dripping from the arm, reaching for her. She fired the .45, into his face, once, twice, then a third time.

She edged back across the ice, the gun held out ahead of her, toward the pulp of face, as if coming in contact with his flesh would disease her. "Bastard," she screamed.

She heard Tildie's whinnie, then rolled onto her belly, reaching out for the AR-15, pulling it toward her, firing it out at the others as they charged toward her. The rifle empty, she stopped firing and slung it across her back, as she reached up for Tildie's stirrup. Then she pulled herself to her feet, snatched at the mane and the saddle horn, and swung up, Tildie wheeling under her, rearing, then coming down. Sarah leveled the .45, firing once, twice, a third time, into her attackers; the slide locked open, empty.

"Gyaagh!" she shouted. Tildie spurred ahead as Sarah tugged at her mane. The animal reared again, wheeled, then streaked off. In the distance, Sarah could see

Michael and Annie, Sam's black mane swatting at Michael's face as he leaned low over the animal's neck, Annie hanging on to his back.

Sarah leaned against Tildie. "Take me out of here," she cooed, feeling tears streaming down her face. "Take me out of here," she said again.

Chapter 10

This was not for the greater glory of mother Russia, he decided. As Major Borozeni stepped inside the abandoned farmhouse, he thought he heard the scurrying sounds of rats. He turned to his sergeant, saying, "Krasny, get a detail in here to clean this place; I do not sleep with rats."

"Yes, Comrade Major." The sergeant saluted.

Borozeni merely nodded, then stepped back outside into the cold. His men were retreating, consolidating their position. The eastern coastal regions of the United States were being buffeted by freak storms. Rebellion was starting everywhere along the southeast coast since the escape, in Savannah, of the Resistance fighters, led by the woman who had bluffed her way through, with him. He felt a smile cross his cracked lips as he dusted snow from the front of his greatcoat; then he pulled away his gloves and felt under the coat for his cigarettes.

"All is being prepared, Comrade Major," Sergeant Krasny told him, saluting as a squad of men with hand torches went past Borozeni into the farmhouse.

"She was quite a woman, Krasny."

"Comrade Major?"

"The woman who effected that escape. I would like to meet her again, see what she looks like without a submachine gun or a pistol in her hands. Or when she isn't all wet, for that matter."

"Yes, Comrade Major."

"Yes." He nodded, walking to keep his feet from freezing. Despite the cold he liked the prospects of the farmhouse even less than the storm. He was to take his contingent of men to Knoxville, Tennessee. He wondered precisely what was in Knoxville; there had been a World's Fair there once, he seemed to recall. He had been on detached duty then, training guerrilla fighters in the Middle East.

He decided he should have been somewhere else. He had never like the Middle East, though he could have used some of its heat now.

The other woman in the truck had used her name. "Sarah," he said, rolling the name on his tongue, tasting it. She was probably someone's wife, perhaps one of the prisoners, who had been released, but he didn't think so. Perhaps someone's widow—one of the men who had been executed.

But then, he asked himself, inhaling deeply on the cigarette, wouldn't she have killed him—a Russian who was an officer, one of the ones responsible for the war?

He threw the cigarette into the snow. She was probably safe in her husband's arms by now . . . or perhaps not.

He felt himself smiling. The trek across the snow, the stalling vehicles, the ice, the freezing temperatures . . . They were somewhere in South Carolina; he didn't remember the name of the town that would be ahead.

He lit another cigarette. He watched the flame of his lighter dancing against the blue whiteness of the ground. "Sarah," he murmured again. The sort of woman he had always wanted to meet—and never would again . . .

He shook his head, smiled, and turned, starting toward the farmhouse. "Krasny! How goes the detail?"

Chapter 11

Natalia studied the map—another half-day if the weather were to ease and they would be in central Indiana. She could convince Paul to leave her there. She looked more intently at the map; she had heard the sound again, beyond the ground-cloth windbreak.

Reaching up to the bootlaces that secured the sleeping bag about her like a coat, she undid them. Finding the flap of the right holster on her belt, she opened it slowly to reduce the noise of the snap in the stillness that was only punctuated by the howling of the wind.

The wood grips felt cold against her bare hand. She glanced at Rubenstein, sleeping, debating whether to awaken him. But if the sound were nothing it would only further convince him he had to take her all the way into northern Indiana. She wanted him back with John Rourke, helping Rourke in the search for his wife and children, helping to keep Rourke alive—for herself?

She shook her head; then extracted the revolver from the holster. It and the one like it on her left hip were curious guns. On the right faces of their slab-sided barrels were engraved American Eagles. The guns were

79

originally four-inch stainless steel Smith & Wesson Model 686s, the .357 Magnum L-frame. On the left flats of the barrels were duplicate inscriptions: METALIFE INDUSTRIES, RENO, PA.—BY RON MAHOVSKY. The actions were the smoothest she had ever felt on a gun; the revolvers were round butted, polished, tuned, perfect. Rourke, when they had been given to her, told her he had known the maker of the guns well before the Night of the War. They would be the best guns she would ever own.

The American Eagles. Mahovsky had made them for President Sam Chambers before the war, and Chambers, for her part in the evacuation of Florida, had insisted she take them. She smiled at the memory, recalling his words. "I can't very well give a Russian spy an American medal, can I? And anyway, we're fresh out of medals. Take these and use 'em to stay alive with, miss."

She had taken them, and the holsters Chambers had had for them; Rourke had found her a belt that better matched her waist size.

She heard the noise again; it snapped her out of her thoughts. She extracted the second revolver now, gloves off, edging up to her feet. She prodded Rubenstein with her left foot; the man rolled over, looking up at her. She raised a finger to her lips, then pointed to her ear.

Rubenstein blinked his eyes, then nodded, suppressing a yawn. He edged back from the fire, the battered Browning High Power he carried coming into his right hand, the hammer slowly cocking back. In the stillness against the wind, it sounded loud—too loud.

She gestured to Paul with one of the guns—that she would cross around behind the bridge support and look. He nodded; he was sensible, she thought. He wore no boots, but she did, and there wasn't time for an alternate plan. The sleeping bag fell from her shoulders and she held the pistol in her left hand against her abdomen, flat, to keep her coat closed more tightly about her.

She shook her head; the wind caught her hair as she stepped out of the crude lean-to into the night. Brigands were her worry—Russian soldiers she could take care of. She had her identification, spoke Russian, could prove who she was and lie about who Paul was.

But Brigands . . . that had been the risk they had run lighting a fire; but otherwise, Paul's feet might have been gone. Frostbite, left untreated, could so quickly turn gangrenous. She didn't want that for Paul—death or being crippled. A friend was too hard a thing to find. Whatever happened, the fire had been worth it, necessary.

She froze, her back flattening against the concrete bridge support as she heard the sound again, this time more clearly—a voice, whispering, meaning there was a second person—at least—in the darkness of the storm.

She stayed against the bridge support, cold, both pistols in her hands, waiting.

They were shiny for night work, but she liked them, the polished stainless steel, the permanence of it—"Permanence," she whispered to herself. What was permanent these days? She had just said good-by to a man whom she had told she loved, a man she would never see again, never forget. And soon, it would be good-by to Paul as well, her friend.

She tried to remember who her friends had been.

Tatiana from her ballet class—they had traded secrets. Tatiana had been Jewish, like Paul; and Tatiana's father had done something—Natalia had never known what— and Tatiana had never returned to ballet class again.

Natalia tried to remember her own parents, but it was impossible. She was only able to remember what her uncle who had raised her had told her about them. Her father had been a doctor, as John was a doctor. Her mother had been a ballerina—they had died. Her Uncle Ishmael had never really fully explained how.

She wondered, silently, whether, when she died, those who cared would know at all.

She didn't think so.

She heard noise again; this time, not the noise of speech, but the bolt of a weapon—assault rifle or submachine gun, she couldn't tell which—being opened.

Perhaps it was Paul with the gun he insisted on calling a Schmeisser, his MP-40.

But the sound had been from the wrong direction.

She bunched her fists around the finger-grooved Goncalo Alves wood grips of the matched Smith & Wessons, then stepped away from the bridge support. She walked, slowly but evenly, toward the edge of the support. She looked around it—she could see the glow of the fire from beyond the far side of the ground-cloth windbreak.

And she could see four men—men or women she wasn't really sure. She had shot both in her lifetime.

They were closing in on the windbreak, in a narrowing circle, assault rifles in their hands. She imagined there were others, behind her, coming up on Paul from the rear. He would have to look out for them—his instincts were good. She would be otherwise engaged.

She stepped away from the bridge support, the glow of the fire glinting off the polished stainless-steel revolvers in her fists.

"What do you want?" she shouted.

One of the nearer assault rifle-armed figures turned toward her. "Ever'thin' you got, li'l gal." He laughed.

"You shouldn't laugh," she said calmly. The man wheeled the muzzle of his rifle toward her, and both pistols bucked at once in her hands. The man's body hammered backward into the snow. The assault rifle discharged, its muzzle flashes lighting up the night, as the second nearer man started to turn, to fire. She caught the sight of hair; it wasn't a man, but a woman. Natalia fired the pistol in her left hand, then the one in her right. The body of the woman twisted and contorted as it fell, her assault rifle impacting into the snow beside her.

Gunfire was coming from the other two and Natalia dove for cover behind a pile of discarded sewer pipes to her left. Bullets whined in the frigid air as they ricocheted off the concrete. Natalia's right hand flashed up, snapping off one shot, then another.

Dumping the empties and the two unfired rounds from the right-hand revolver into her right palm as she stroked the ejector rod, she huddled behind the pipes; the gunfire coming more steadily now. In a pocket of her coat she had a half-dozen Safariland Speed Loaders. She snatched them, ramming the bullets into the charging holes, the center of the loader actuating against the ejector star, the cases freed and spilling into the charging holes. She slammed the cylinder shut, fired the gun in her left hand—four shots, a scream.

There was more gunfire.

Then from her far right, she heard the small-caliber, high-pitched belching of the Schmeisser. "Paul," she said.

She speed-loaded the revolver for her left hand, then holstered it, the gun in her right hand firing as she pushed herself up, running from the concrete sewer pipes toward the bridge support, firing at the nearer of the two assault rifle-armed figures. The body went down, its gun still firing. "Wounded," she murmured. Whoever Paul had been shooting at was on the far side of the bridge support. And Paul's gun had stopped firing.

She reached the lean-to. Rubenstein was locked in combat with three men. She heard Paul's subgun discharge though she couldn't see it; one of the men fell back, stumbling into the fire, his body and clothes now aflame. Natalia fired her revolver once into the man's head to put him out of his agony. Then having taken two steps closer to Paul, she half-turned, balancing in the snow on her right foot. Her left foot snaked out, giving a double savate kick to the head of the nearest of the two remaining men.

The man fell back against the bridge support, and she could see Paul now, his right arm bound up in the sling for his subgun, his left hand holding back the knife of his opponent, clutched around the man's right wrist.

The subgun fell away; Paul's right fist hammered up, into the midsection of the vastly larger man.

Natalia's instincts told her something.

She wheeled, emptying the revolver in her right hand into two men charging for her. She wheeled again. No time for the revolver in her left hand, she dropped the Metalife Custom L-Frame from her right fist, snatching in the same motion for the Bali-Song knife in the right side hip pocket of her jump suit.

Her thumb flicked open the lock as her right arm hauled back. The closed knife sailed from her grip as she threw her arm forward. From beyond the windbreak, a man advanced against her with an assault rifle. The stainless-steel Bali-Song glinted in the firelight as it rotated in the air, the handle halves splitting open.

The man with the assault rifle stopped in his tracks, both hands out at his sides, the rifle falling from his grip. The handle slabs of her knife were flat against the front of his coat, making a horizontal line. The body sagged, then fell forward, into the fire, and Natalia, as she snatched the revolver from her left holster, could smell his flesh burning on the wind.

Rubenstein! She could see him, his left hand still locked on the knife wrist of the man he fought. Suddenly his right arm hauled back, then flashed forward, his bunched-together right fist smashing into the nose of the larger man. The man's knife hand went limp; the knife fell.

As the man fell back, Rubenstein snatched at the pistol from his belt, firing the High Power almost point-blank into the man's midsection as the body stumbled, then collapsed.

"Two outside, maybe," she snapped, the revolver sailing from her left hand into her right as she rounded the edge of the bridge support.

She ran hard, reaching the far side, making the corner. An assault rifle at the shoulder of one of the two men there started opening up, its flashes blinding against the snowy darkness. She stabbed the revolver forward in her hands and double-actioned it twice. The man's head shuddered under the impact of the slugs, his body falling, as the assault rifle fired uselessly up into the night sky.

She wheeled. Firing the L-Frame again at the last of the two, she heard the chattering of Paul's submachine gun as well. The body of the last of the attackers rolled, twisted, lurched under the impact of the slugs hammering at it; then it was still. "Too bad," she said.

She heard Paul's voice. "Yeah—what a waste of human life."

"That, too," she told him. "But with all the bullet holes, none of their coats will do us much good for added warmth." She started back toward the windbreak, saying, "Check that they're all dead while I get my other gun and the knife." She felt very cold, and realized Paul probably thought her colder. "If any of them aren't dead—tell me," she added.

She sat down, picking up her gun, not yet ready mentally to retrieve the Bali-Song knife. The gun was undamaged. Automatically, she emptied the revolver of the spent cases, then reloaded it with one of the remaining Speedloaders. She loaded the second revolver as well, holstering both guns; then, her hands trembling, she lit a cigarette.

"Tired!" she screamed.

Chapter 12

John Rourke looked at the Rolex; the exterior of the crystal was steamed so he smudged it away with his right glove, then studied the time. It was eight-thirty. A good time for a party, he thought—the shank of the evening.

He leaned against the pine trunk, staring down into the valley, the wind behind him now, the sweater pulled down from covering his head, his leather jacket unzipped and wide open. The Bushnell Armored 8X30s focused under his hands as he swept them across the valley floor. A town—a perfect town, nothing changed. A blue-grass band was playing in the town square, strains of the music barely audible in the distance; children played behind a crowd of spectators surrounding the band; a car moved along the far side of the town, its lights setting a pattern of zigzags in the shadows where the streetlights didn't hit.

For an instant only, Rourke questioned his own sanity, then dismissed the idea.

He was sane; it was what he saw that wasn't sane.

He took out one of his dark tobacco cigars, rolling it across his mouth between his teeth to the left corner, then letting the Bushnell binoculars dangle down from the strap around his neck. He found his lighter, and flicking the Zippo, touched the tip of the cigar nearly into the flame. Drawing, he felt the smoke in his lungs as he inhaled.

He and Natalia and Paul had often talked about it—a world gone mad; but beneath him now, on the valley floor, was a world that hadn't changed. Was that madness? He closed his eyes, listening to the music. . . .

Comfortable with his leather jacket open—he would have worn it now if he had been hot because it concealed the twin stainless Detonics .45s—he rode the Harley into the town, his Python and the hip holster hidden in his pack, the CAR-15 still wrapped in the blanket. At least it would take a reasonably knowledgeable curious person to determine that it was a gun.

He could hear the music more clearly now as he passed a small school; the facility would handle perhaps three hundred students, he decided. From the high ground inside the lip of the valley, he had seen most of the town in relief against the valley floor, but the details had been lost. Now he could see it more clearly. No evidence of looting, bombing, fires—nothing that showed there had ever been a war. The Night of the War hadn't touched this place.

He felt like Hilton's very British hero, entering Shangri-La and leaving the storm behind him.

"The storm," he whispered to himself. Both literally and figuratively, a storm.

He stopped his Harley-Davidson Low Rider for a stop sign; a police car was across from him at the other side of the four-way stop.

Rourke ran his fingers through his hair, then gave the cop a wave and a nod as he started. The police prowl car moved slowly, the policeman lighting his dome light, looking but saying nothing as Rourke passed the vehicle.

Rourke chewed down on the burned out stub of his cigar now. Reaching the end of a storybook residential street, he turned left after slowing for a yield sign, a public library on his right as he started toward the lights of the square. A young girl wearing a dress sat on the steps of the library building, with a boy of the same age sitting beside her, the two talking.

The boy looked up, and Rourke gave him a nod, driving on. He passed the post office; the street angled slightly toward the town square.

He stopped the Harley beside the curb, staring at what he saw. It was just as he'd seen it from above—a band playing, some younger people dancing, clogging or step-dancing, children running and playing, some tugging on their mothers—perhaps two hundred people in all around the square.

He turned off the key for the Harley. He couldn't help himself as he sat there, listening to the music, but hearing different music—a song he and Sarah had always called their own song, danced to so many times. In the faces of the strange children, Rourke saw the faces of his own. What he couldn't stop, what he felt—tears—a world gone.

Had Sarah seen him, he smiled, she would have thought he was almost human. . . .

The blue-grass band had stopped, and a record player was humming through the loudspeakers; there was the scratching sound of a needle against plastic, then a country song, and through a momentary niche in the wall of humanity surrounding the center of the square he saw more children—girls in green-and-white plaid dresses with short skirts and petticoats that made the skirts stand away from their legs, the oldest of the girls perhaps twelve, the youngest looking to be Annie's age—five or so.

Boys in green slacks and white shirts and green bow ties—only a few boys though—stood beside them, all in a rank. They started dancing; clogging, it was called.

Rourke smelled something, then turned and looked to his right. A gleaming truck, the kind that would come to factories to bring coffee and doughnuts and hamburgers, was parked at the edge of the square.

He saw a sign above the open side that formed a counter—the sign read, COKE.

Rourke walked toward the truck. A little girl passed him, coming from the truck, a half-eaten hot dog in her right hand, yellow mustard around her mouth and dribbling down her chin.

Rourke automatically felt his pockets. He still carried his money clip—but was there anything in it? "Yes," he murmured. Something just hadn't made him give away or throw away money. He pulled out a ten and walked over to the truck.

"What'll ya' have, mister?"

"Ahh—two hot dogs and a Coke. Make it three hot dogs."

"You new in town, ain't ya? Related to anyone 'round here?"

"What's the occasion?" Rourke asked, something making him evade the question. He jerked his thumb toward the town square behind him.

"It's the Fourth of July, mister. Ain't you got no calendar?"

"I—I've been camping—up in the mountains. Kind of lost track of time."

90

"I reckon you have." The man smiled, handing Rourke the three hot dogs in a small white cardboard box. Rourke handed him the ten-dollar bill and took the Coke, then started away.

"Hey!"

Rourke turned around.

"You forgot your change!"

"Keep it," Rourke told him. "Maybe I'll want another hot dog later." Rourke turned and spat his cigar butt into a trash can near him. He walked across the square a short way, finding a tree and leaning against it, listening to the music, seeing the children clog. He took a bite from the hot dog nearest him in the box, the Coke set down beside him on the ground. It wasn't near the Fourth of July.

The man who had sold him the hot dogs wasn't from here, either—he had said "you" not "y'all" and that went with the territory. Rourke had made the speech pattern as midwestern.

Maybe it was the Russians—something that would be a trap. But for whom? The town, the dancing, the Fourth of July. If he wasn't crazy, all of them were.

He wasn't crazy, he reminded himself, feeling the comfort of his guns under his jacket as he nudged his upper arms against his body. "I'm not crazy," he verbalized. The hot dog had tasted good and he started to eat the second one, dismissing any worry it was drugged. The little girl was dancing around, helping the cloggers; the only thing apparently wrong with her being terminal mustard stains. . . .

Rourke sipped at his Coke—it was real Coca-Cola. He hadn't had any since— He worked along the perimeter of the crowd, watching the faces, the genuine smiles. He nudged against a man and the man turned, smiled, and said, "Hey!"

It was the universal southern greeting that Rourke had learned long ago as a transplanted northerner.

"Hi." Rourke smiled, as the man turned away to watch the clogging. This was a second group of cloggers, dressed the same but in red and white rather than green and white. The green- and white-clad girls and boys stood at the edge of the crowd now, watching the others.

Rourke saw a face; it was the only face not smiling. It looked promising, he thought, and gravitated toward the woman belonging to it.

As he neared the woman, the clogging stopped—abruptly—and an announcer, a fat man wearing a red-and white-checkered cowboy shirt and a straw cowboy hat, said through the microphone, "Let's give these little folks a big, big hand!" Rourke held his cup in his teeth a moment and applauded, then kept moving toward the woman with the unsmiling face.

Slower country music started to play and the crowd started splitting up. Rourke cut easily through the wave of people now, some of them gravitating toward the edge of the square, some pairing off and dancing to the music. The woman with the unsmiling face apparently wasn't with anyone; she turned and started away. Rourke downed the rest of his Coke and tossed the cup into a trash can nearby, then called out to her. "Hey—ahh." The woman turned around.

Rourke stopped, a few feet from her, saying, "I, ahh—"

"Y'all want to dance?" she smiled.

"All right." Rourke nodded, stepping closer to her.

She slung her handbag in the crook of her left arm on its straps. Rourke took her right hand in his left, his right

92

arm encircling her waist. She was about forty, pretty enough, but not a woman who seemed to try to be pretty at all.

Her face was smiling, but not her eyes.

"Who are you?" She smiled, coming into his arms.

"John—my name's John," he told her.

"You're carrying a gun, John," she whispered, her head close to his chest. "I read a lot of detective stories. I'm the librarian. I know."

"You oughta read more," he told her softly. "I'm carrying two."

"Ohh—all right, John."

"Hasn't anyone heard about World War III here?" he asked her, smiling as they danced their way nearer the blue-grass band.

"If anyone else heard you mention the war, John, the same thing would happen to you that happened to all the rest of them. We'll talk later, at my place."

"Ohh." Rourke nodded. He wondered who the rest of them had been. As he held the woman's hand when they danced, he automatically felt her pulse; it was rapid and strong. . . .

Chapter 13

Nehemiah Rozhdestvenskiy stepped down from the aircraft to the sodden tarmac of the runway surface. "The weather—it is insane," he shouted to the KGB man with him.

"Yes, Comrade Colonel." The man nodded, offering an umbrella, but the rain—chillingly cold—had already soaked him, and Rozhdestvenskiy watched, almost amused, as a strong gust of wind caught up the umbrella and turned it inside out.

He shook his head, and ran through the puddles toward the waiting automobile. He read the name on it as he entered. "Suburban." He ran the name through his head—it was a type of Chevrolet. . . .

The ride had taken longer than Rozhdestvenskiy had anticipated because he had been unable to use a helicopter. But as the large Chevy wagon stopped, he felt himself smiling—it had been worth the wait.

There was already a searchlight trained on the massive bombproof doors—they *had* been bombproof at least. They were wide apart now, gaping into darkness beyond.

"Mt. Lincoln," Rozhdestvenskiy murmured. The presidential retreat.

He stepped out and down, into the mud.

"Comrade Colonel," the solicitous officer, who had tried the umbrella, said as he joined Rozhdestvenskiy in the mud.

"It is all right, Voskavich—do not trouble over the mud. The facility is secured?"

"Yes, Comrade Colonel—there were no prisoners." The KGB officer smiled.

"I wanted prisoners."

"They were all dead when we arrived, Comrade. A fault in the air-circulation system. The bodies, were, ahh . . ." The younger man let the sentence hang.

"Very well—they were all dead, then." Rozhdestvenskiy dismissed the idea. "We will enter—it is safe to do so then?"

"Yes, Comrade Colonel." He extracted from under his raincoat two gas masks.

"This is for—"

"The bodies, Comrade Colonel—they have not all been removed as yet and—"

"I understand." Rozhdestvenskiy nodded. He ran his fingers through his soaking hair as he started toward the entrance, nodding only at salutes—he was dressed in civilian clothes—and stopping before the steel doors. "You were able to penetrate these?"

"One of the particle-beam weapons ordered here by the late Colonel Karamatsov, Comrade. It was brought here for this purpose I presume?"

"Partly. It is sensitive material that we cannot discuss here in the open. It was efficient," Rozhdestvenskiy said, looking at the doors and feeling genuinely impressed. The entire central section of both doors looked to have been vaporized.

He ran his fingers through his hair again, pulled on the gas mask, and popped the cheeks, blowing out to seal it; then he started forward with a hand torch given him by the younger KGB officer. Through the gas mask, hearing the odd sound of his own voice, he said, "You will lead the way for me, Voskavich."

"Yes, Comrade Colonel." The younger man was a captain and Rozhdestvenskiy decided that the man had no intention of remaining one.

"You have done well, Voskavich. Rest assured, your superiors are aware of your efficiency."

"Thank you, Comrade," the younger man enthused. "Be careful here, Comrade—a wet spot and you might slip."

Rozhdestvenskiy nodded, staring ahead of them. There was a lagoon; or at least there appeared to be one in the darkness of the massive cave inside the mountain.

"We have boats, Comrade Colonel. The Americans used them I believe to inspect the lagoon and we must use them to cross it. This was a service entrance and the most direct route to the presidential suite is—"

"I know, Voskavich; I, too, have read these plans until they were something I dreamed about. We shall take one of the boats—Charon." Rozhdestvenskiy laughed at his own joke—the boatman to take him across the river Styx.

But Voskavich was not the boatman; another KGB man, a sergeant, was running the small outboard. Rozhdestvenskiy climbed aboard from the lagoon shoreline, reassessing his nomenclature in terms of the American language. This would not be a lagoon, but rather a lake because of its progressively greater depth. A man-made lake? he wondered. None of his readings of intelligence reports dealing with Mt. Lincoln had ever indicated the origin of the waters there.

There was a small spotlight jury-rigged to the helm of the large rowboat; and between that and the flashlights both Rozhdestvenskiy and Voskavich held, there was ample light to see the even surface of the waters. At its widest, Rozhdestvenskiy judged the lake to be perhaps three-quarters of a mile across. He leaned back as best he could; he liked boat rides, despite wearing the gas mask, despite the lighting. When he someday returned a hero to the Soviet Union, he had decided, he would get a boat and a house on the Black Sea. There were many beautiful women there, and somehow beautiful women seemed especially fond of influential KGB officers.

And influential he would be if he were able to solidify all the speculations regarding the Eden Project, and thereby eliminate this last potential U.S. threat. He favored the most popular theory—that the Eden Project was a doomsday device. The Americans had always been kind and careful people so if they had a doomsday device encircling the globe now, there would be some way of deactivating it in the event it had been launched by mistake. He would find that way of deactivating it, then be the hero.

It was simple.

He even knew where to look for the plans for the device. Part of Mt. Lincoln held a filing room containing duplicates of the most highly classified war-related documents, for the reference of the president. It was there that this most classified of documents would be kept—there that he would find his answer.

Rozhdestvenskiy felt the motorized rowboat bump against the far shore of the lake. The ride was over. . . .

*   *   *

Rozhdestvenskiy felt like a graverobber, like an unscrupulous archeologist invading the tomb of a once-great Pharaoh—and perhaps it was a Pharaoh's tomb, the tomb of the last real president of the United States. He discounted this Chambers; he had taken the power, but by all reports from the late quisling Randan Soames, Chambers had taken the power reluctantly. The power had not been given him as it was to other American presidents—such a strange custom, Rozhdestvenskiy thought as he shone the light of the torch across the gaping mouth of a partially decomposed U.S. Marine. To hold free elections and trust the mass of the people to select a leader who was accountable to them.

"No wonder they didn't prevail," Rozhdestvenskiy murmured.

Voskavich asked, "Comrade Colonel?"

"The Americans—their absurd ideas of doing things—it accounts handily for their failure." The thought crossed his mind, though, that Soviet troops were now retreating to regroup for the fight against American Resistance on the eastern seaboard. Their failure had not yet been completely recognized.

Voskavich stepped across the body of the dead Marine, saying, "These men were trapped here—perhaps locked inside."

"That is not the American way. They were probably happy to have died in the service of their country. Give the devil his due, Voskavich." Rozhdestvenskiy picked his way over the bodies, seeing ahead of him at the end of a long corridor what he thought was the room.

It recalled the Egyptian tomb analogy to his mind—these Marines, priests of the order, guardians of the Pharaoh, who was their high priest. The priests of Democracy—an outmoded religion, Rozhdestvenskiy thought. But he did not smile. Despite himself, he was saddened to see the death masks of these priests, the anguish, the sorrow, the shock. He wondered what loved ones they had left behind, what dreams they had held dear. They were young, all of them, these priests.

He stopped before the "temple." There was a combination lock on the vaultlike doors. "I shall need experts in this sort of thing—immediately," Rozhdestvenskiy ordered.

"Yes, Comrade Colonel," Voskavich answered, starting to leave. The younger man paused, turning to Rozhdestvenskiy. "Should I leave you here, Comrade?"

"The dead cannot hurt me," Rozhdestvenskiy told him. Voskavich left then and Rozhdestvenskiy stood amid the bodies, by the sealed doors, studying the faces.

In not one of them could he find disillusionment. They had died for something important—what was it? Rozhdestvenskiy wondered. . . .

A sergeant, a corporal and two lieutenants had labored over the locking system of the doors, for more than a half hour, and now Voskavich turned to him, saying, "Comrade Colonel—they are ready."

Rozhdestvenskiy only nodded, then touched his black-gloved right hand to the door handle, twisting it. Pulling it open toward him, he shone his light inside. He felt like Carter at the discovery of Tutankhamen. No golden idols were here, but file cabinets, unopened, unlike the ones in other parts of the complex. There was no pile of charred papers and microfilm rolls in the center of the floor.

"No tomb robbers have beaten us," he remarked,

then stepped inside. He walked quickly through the darkness, the light of his torch showing across the yellow indexes on the file drawers.

He found the one he wanted—the ones. There were six file drawers marked "Project 4,832-C/RS9." He opened the top drawer to pull out the abstract sheets at the front of the file. He read them, then closed his eyes, suddenly very tired.

"Voskavich, these drawers are not to be looked in. I will need carts for removing the contents after they have been boxed. Bring the cartons here and I will do that personally."

"Yes, Comrade Colonel Rozhdestvenskiy," Voskavich answered.

"Leave me here—alone." And Rozhdestvenskiy, when the last one of them had left, switched off his torch and stood in the darkness beside the file drawers. He knew now what the Eden Project was. The Americans never ceased to amaze him.

Chapter 14

"I wasn't born here. Most of the rest of them were, and their parents were born here, too, and before that," the woman told him.

"What the hell does that mean, lady?" Rourke asked her, exasperated, smiling as he spoke through tightly clenched teeth while the men and women and children of the town who had made up the knot of humanity in the town square were now breaking up, going home.

"My name's Martha Bogen." She smiled.

"My question wasn't about your name. Don't these people—"

"That's right, Abe." She smiled, saying the last words loudly, a knot of people coming up to them, stopping. She looked at a pretty older woman at the center of a group of people roughly in their sixties, Rourke judged. She said, "Marion—this is my brother, Abe Collins. He finally made it here to join me!"

"Ohh," the older woman cooed. "Martha, we're so happy for you—to have your brother with you. Ohh—Abe," she said, extending a hand Rourke took. The hand was clammy and cold. "It's so wonderful to meet you after all this time. Martha's younger brother. I hope we'll see you in church tomorrow."

"Well, I had a hard ride. . . . I'll try though." Rourke smiled.

"Good! I know you and Martha have so much to talk about." The older woman smiled again.

Rourke was busy shaking hands with the others, and as they left, he smiled broadly at Martha Bogen, his right hand clamping on her upper left arm, the fingers boring tightly into her flesh. "You give me some answers—now."

"Walk me home, Abe, and I'll try." She smiled, the smile genuine, Rourke thought.

"I'll get my bike; it's at the corner." He gestured toward it, half-expecting that in the instant since he'd last looked for it someone had taken it. But it was there, untouched. "I suppose you've got a fully operational gas station, too?"

"Yes. You can fill up tomorrow. You should stay here tonight—at my house. Everyone will expect it."

"Why?" Rourke rasped.

"I told them you were my brother—of course." She smiled again, taking his arm and starting with him through the ever-thinning crowd.

"Why did you tell them that?"

"If they knew you were a stranger, then they'd have to do something." She smiled, nodding to another old lady as they passed her.

Rourke smiled and nodded, too, then rasped, "Do what?"

"The strangers—most of them didn't want to stay."

"Nobody's going to think I'm your brother. That was so damned transparent—"

"My brother was coming. He's probably dead out there

102

like everybody else. God knows how you survived."

"A lot of us survived—not everyone's dead."

"I know that, but it must be terrible out there—a world like that."

"They know I'm not your brother."

"I know they do," Martha Bogen said, "but it won't matter—so long as you pretend."

Rourke shook his head, looking at her, saying, his voice low, "Pretend—what the hell is going on here?"

"I can't explain it well enough for you to understand, Abe—"

"It's John. I told you that."

"John. Walk me home, then just sleep on the couch; it looks like there's bad weather outside the valley tonight. Then tomorrow with a good meal in you—not just those terrible hot dogs—well, you can decide what you want to do."

Rourke stopped beside his bike. "I won't stay—not now," he told her, the hairs on the back of his neck standing up, telling him something more than he could imagine was wrong.

"Did you see the police on the way into town—John?"

"So what?" He looked at her.

"They let anyone in, but they won't let you out. And at night you won't stand a chance unless you know the valley. I know the valley. Before he died, my husband used to take me for long walks. He hunted the valley a lot—white-tailed deer. I know every path there is."

Rourke felt the corners of his mouth downturning. "How long ago did your husband die?"

"He was a doctor. You have hands like a doctor, John. Good hands. He died five years ago. There was an influenza outbreak in the valley and he worked himself half to death; children, pregnant women—all of them had it. And he caught it and he died."

"I'm sorry, Martha," Rourke told her genuinely. "But I can't stay."

"We have twelve policemen and they work twelve-hour shifts lately—six men on and six off. Can you fight twelve policemen to get out of town—into a storm?" She stroked his face with her right hand. "You need a shave. I'll bet a hot shower would be good, and a warm bed."

Her face flushed, then she added, "In the guest room, I meant."

Rourke nodded. There was no strategic reserve site for more than a hundred miles, and Rourke knew that he needed gasoline. The slow going in the storm had depleted his tanks. "That gas station really has gas?" he asked her.

"You can even use my credit card, John, if you don't have any money."

Rourke looked at her, speechless. "Credit card?" The gasoline—without it he couldn't press the search for Sarah and the children. "All right, Martha, I'll accept your generous invitation. Thank you." His skin crawled when he said it.

Chapter 15

Tildie's breath came in clouds of heavy steam. On a rise overlooking Lake Hartwell, Sarah reined the sweating animal in. Beneath her horse's hoofs was South Carolina and on the far shore, Georgia. In the distance, to her left, she could make out the giant outline of the dam through the swirling snow. And below her, on the lake, was a large flat-bottomed houseboat. Smoke drifted from a small chimney in the center of the houseboat's roof. She looked behind her at Michael and Annie, freezing with the cold; at Sam, John's horse before the war and now she supposed more realistically Michael's horse. The animal was shuddering as large clouds of steam, like those Tildie exhaled, gushed from its nostrils.

"Michael, where'd you get that knife?"

"One of the children on the island—he gave it to me."

Sarah didn't know what to say. Her son had just stabbed at a man trying to hurt him, trying to hurt his sister. "You did the right thing, using it—but be careful with it." She couldn't quite bring herself to tell him that she wanted to take it away from him. "Just be careful with it. We'll talk about it later."

"All right," he said—slightly defensively, she thought.

Sarah looked at the houseboat again. "I'm going to see if there's anyone aboard that houseboat—if maybe we can find shelter with them. Michael, you and Annie stay here. Don't come after me. If it looks like I'm in trouble . . . then . . ." She didn't know what to tell him. Finally she said, "Use your own judgment. But wait until I come for you or you see I'm in trouble. Understood?"

"Yes, I understand," he told her.

She knew he understood; whether he would do as she asked was another question. "And watch out behind you—for those people." She didn't know what else to call the wild men and women who had attacked them.

She stepped down from Tildie, her rear end suddenly cold from leaving the built-up warmth of the saddle. She handed Michael Tildie's reins. "Hold her. I'm going down there to look."

Sarah settled the AR-15 across her back, on its sling, then thought better of it. She took the rifle off and held it in her right hand, a fresh thirty-round magazine in place, the chamber loaded already. Her pistol, John's pistol, was freshly reloaded and back against her abdomen under her clothes. It was starting to rust a great deal; she didn't know what to do to stop it except to oil the gun.

With her gloved left hand she tugged at the blue-and-white bandanna on her hair, pulling it down where it had slipped up from covering her left ear.

She smiled at the children. "I love you both. Michael. Take care of Annie." She started down from the rise, toward the houseboat. It appeared as though there were no moorings, that something like a tide was forcing the boat toward shore.

She hurried as best she could, slipping several times where the iced-over gravel was still loose, the red clay beneath it slick and wet and like polished ice.

When she reached the base of the rise, the houseboat was less than thirty feet away.

There were no mooring lines, but there were trees nearby that would do, she calculated. The houseboat rose and fell with the meager tide, edging in toward the shore and away. Sarah visually searched the bank. At one place the houseboat's gunwales were three feet away from the edge when the flat-bottomed craft drifted in. Sarah skidded down, along the red clay toward this spot, secured her rifle, then waited, wiping imaginary sweat from her palms as she rubbed her gloved hands along her thighs.

The houseboat was easing in. Sarah jumped, her hand reaching out for the line of rope that formed the rail, grabbing at it. The rope, ice-coated, slipped from her fingers.

She twisted her body, arching her back, throwing her weight forward, crashing her arms down across the rope, falling, heaving over the rail and sprawling across the ice-coated deck.

She lay there a moment, catching her breath, her belly aching where the butt of the Government Model Colt had slammed against it as she fell. She rolled onto her side, giving a brave wave toward the children, still watching her from atop the rise. But she didn't call out because of the smoke in the houseboat chimney—there had to be people aboard.

Sarah tried standing up, but the deck was too slippery for her and she fell, catching herself on her hands, the butt of the AR-15 slamming into the deckboards. She crawled on hands and knees toward the door leading inside.

She stopped beside the closed door and reaching around behind her, got the AR-15 and worked the selector to full auto. Reaching up to it, she tried the door handle. It opened under her hand, swinging outside to her left.

Not entering, she looked inside. A man and a woman lay on the bed at the far corner of the large room, the sheets around them stained; the smell assailed her nose. They were locked in each other's arms, their bodies blue-veined and dead.

"They killed themselves," she murmured, resting her head against the doorjamb.

Sarah Rourke wept for them—and for herself.

Chapter 16

Settling his glasses back on the bridge of his nose, Paul Rubenstein pulled down the bandanna covering his face as he slowed the Harley, the snow under it slushy and wet. He looked up, and for a brief instant could see a patch of blue beyond the fast scudding gray clouds.

"It is breaking up," Natalia said from behind him.

"'Bout time." He smiled. He suddenly had the realization of the air temperature on his face. "Must be twenty degrees warmer than it was when we broke camp," he told her, looking over his right shoulder at her.

"We should be getting into my territory soon, Paul—there may not be time," she began

"I know; give John your love, right?"

He felt the Russian woman punch him in the back. "Yes." He heard her laugh. "And this is for you." And he felt her hands roughly twisting his head around, her face bumped his glasses as she kissed him full on the lips. "I won't ask you to give that to John—that was for you." She smiled.

"Look, you don't have to—"

"To go back to my people? John and I went over that. I have to. I'm a Russian—no matter how good my English

109

is, no matter how much I can sound or look like an American. I'm a Russian. What I feel for John, what I feel for you as my friend—that will never change. But being what I am won't change either."

"You know you're fighting on the wrong side," Rubenstein told her, suddenly feeling himself not smiling.

"If I said the same thing to you, would you believe me? I don't mean believe that I believed it, but believe it inside yourself?"

"No," Rubenstein said flatly.

"Then the same answer for you, Paul. No. My people have done a great deal of harm, but so have yours. With good men like my uncle, perhaps I can do something— to—"

"Make the world safe for Communism?" He laughed.

She laughed, too, saying through her laughter, "You're not the same barefoot boy from the Big Apple that I met long ago, Paul."

He was deadly serious when he said to her, "And you're not the same person you pretended to be then. I'll tell you what your problem is. You grew up believing in one set of ideals and you've been realizing what you believed in all that time was wrong. Karamatsov was the Communist, the embodiment of—"

"I won't listen anymore, Paul." She smiled, touching her fingers to his lips.

"All right." He smiled, kissing her forehead as she leaned against his chest for a moment. "Just think what a team you and John would make," he told her then.

She looked up at him, her eyes wet. "Fighting? Always fighting? Brigands or some other enemies?"

"That's not what I meant. You can find other ways to

be invincible together." He laughed because he'd sounded so serious, so philosophical.

"He—he can't. And I can't."

"What if he never finds Sarah?"

"He will," she told him flatly.

Paul said again, "What if he never finds Sarah? Would you marry him?"

"That's none of your business, Paul," she said, then smiled.

"I know it isn't—but would you?"

"Yes," she said softly, then started to fumble in her bag. She took out a cigarette and a lighter, then plunged the tip of the cigarette into the flame with what looked to Rubenstein like a vengeance.

"Stay where you are. Raise your hands and you will not be harmed!"

Rubenstein looked ahead of them—a half-dozen Russian soldiers, greatcoats stained with snow, and at their head a man he guessed was an officer. "You are under arrest. Lay down your arms!"

She said it in English—he guessed so he could understand. "I am Major Natalia Tiemerovna,"—Rubenstein thought he detected her voice catch for an instant before she added, "of the Committee for State Security of the Soviet."

Chapter 17

Varakov pushed the button for his window to roll down—it was warm now, so much warmer than it had been.

He glanced at his driver; this driver was not as good a man as Leon had been. Varakov exhaled hard, waiting as the Soviet fighter bomber taxied across the field.

He decided to get out. "You will wait for me here." He opened the door. "I can get out myself."

"Yes, Comrade General," the driver answered, turning around.

Varakov smiled. There was no reason to act gruffly toward the young man simply because he was not Leon. "You may smoke if you wish, Corporal," Varakov added, stepping outside, then slamming the door.

Varakov snorted, stretched, and started walking toward the slowing-down taxiing aircraft.

Was there a doomsday project that the United States had launched? Was an end finally coming? he asked himself.

He had avoided philosophy—meticulously. Philosophy and generalship were not compatible; they never had been.

He had lived a full life—full because of his achievements, because of the friendships he had made, because of the daughter he had raised—not his daughter, but his brother's daughter, Natalia.

He had done that well, he thought. The thing with Karamatsov behind her, she would grow away from it. She would meet another man. Or had she met him already, the American Rourke?

He shook his head.

He worried over Natalia, and the people like her, the new Russia he had fought all his life to make survive, to make triumphant. "Doomsday," he murmured, thinking once again about the Eden Project.

The plane stopped, the passengers' doorway opening immediately. Uniformed Soviet soldiers rolled a ramp toward it; and already framed in the doorway, civilian clothes as rumpled as though he had slept in them, his blond hair tousled in the breeze, stood Rozhdestvenskiy.

Varakov walked the few extra yards toward the foot of the steps. Rozhdestvenskiy was already halfway down them.

"Did you learn anything, Colonel?"

The younger man stopped. "I learned it all, Comrade General—all of it." Then he turned away for an instant, to shout up into the plane. "Those six cartons of documents—the seals are to remain untouched, unbroken. They are to be delivered to my car—immediately."

Varakov glanced down the airfield. There was a black American Cadillac waiting; and Varakov assumed it was Rozhdestvenskiy's car. As the younger officer reached the base of the steps, Varakov extended his right hand—not in greeting, but to Rozhdestvenskiy's left forearm, to hold him there a moment. "Is there a doomsday device?

113

What is it?"

"Not a device, Comrade General," Rozhdestvenskiy said, not smiling. "And I cannot tell you any more; those are the orders of the Politburo." Then Rozhdestvenskiy added, "I am sorry, sir."

He shrugged off the hand and walked away.

Varakov watched as the first of the red-sealed packing crates was carried down and past him.

The old man's feet hurt.

Chapter 18

Glancing at his Rolex, Rourke wiped the steam of the shower away from the crystal.

It was nearly noon, the woman having let him over-sleep—or perhaps just the fact of sleeping in a bed in a normal-seeming home had done it to him. During the night he had dreamed—about Sarah, about Michael and Annie . . . and about Natalia.

He could not remember the dreams, and he was grateful for that. Dreams were something that could not be controlled, an alien environment that merely happened out of the subconscious. Desires, fears—all of them things he could not manipulate to his own choosing. They had always annoyed him—and if anything did, slightly frightened him.

He turned the water straight cold, the hairs on his chest grayer, he noticed, his body leaner. He shut off the water, opening the shower curtain, snatching the towel, and beginning to dry himself before stepping out into the neat and very feminine-looking bathroom. He glanced once between the shower curtain and the plastic liner; on the lip of the tub was one of his stainless-steel Detonics .45s, none the worse for wear apparently.

He noted the bruise on his shoulder in the partially steamed-over mirror, the bruise from his fall from the plane to the road surface. He flexed that arm to work out the stiffness. It would heal, he diagnosed. He smiled—no doctor worth his salt trusted self-diagnosis, but under the circumstances . . .

Martha Bogen was making him breakfast, despite the hour, so meanwhile Rourke took the Harley from the garage where it had been locked overnight, and following her directions, headed toward the nearest gas station.

He turned the machine now, his hair blowing in the warm breeze coming down the mountain slope, his blue shirt sleeves rolled up, both of the Detonics .45s stuffed inside the waistband of his trousers under the shirt. He could see the gas station ahead. There was one car at the self-service island so Rourke turned to the full-service island, shutting down.

He let out the kickstand and dismounted. A smiling attendant in a blue workshirt with the name, "Al," stitched over the heart came from inside the service bays; there was a car inside getting an oil change.

"Fill 'er up?"

"Yeah. I've got an auxiliary tank—fill that, too," Rourke rasped.

"Check your oil?"

"Yeah. Check my oil." Rourke nodded. He looked at his bike. Miraculously, after the air crash, then the skid on the icy mountain roads, there were no visible scratches, no visible damage.

"Y'all related to someone round here?" The attendant smiled.

Rourke shrugged mentally. "Yeah. My sister's Martha Bogen. My name's Abe."

"Well . . . hey, Abe." The attendant smiled. "I'm happy for Martha. It woulda been sad."

Rourke started to ask why, then nodded. "Yeah—sure would," he agreed.

"Nice lookin' machine y'all got here," Al said.

"Thanks." Rourke nodded. "Nice looking town. Cold as a witch's—Real cold outside. You got funny weather."

"Yeah. Just a little pocket here, I guess. We was always fixin' to get together with them fellers at the National Weather Service and maybe find out why, but never did get around to it."

Pointedly, Rourke said, "Well, there's always tomorrow," and smiled.

"Hey, there you go." Al laughed. "All set." He withdrew the nozzle and started to replace the gas cap. Checking the pump, Rourke reached into his pocket for his money clip. He handed the man a twenty.

"I'll get some—"

"Keep the change." Rourke smiled, remounting the Harley, starting it, and upping the kickstand.

"Say . . . thanks, Abe." Al waved.

"O.K." Rourke nodded. They were all insane, he decided, as he started back into the street. . . .

"You're a good cook," Rourke told her, looking up from the steak and eggs nearly finished on the blue-willow plate in front of him.

"I don't usually get the chance." She smiled. "Living alone and all."

He smiled back at her. "You haven't lost your touch."

She turned back to the sink and shut off the water, then turned back to him, wiping her hands on her apron. "You haven't asked me any questions yet."

"You promised it'd all be made clear. I'm waiting for you, I guess." He smiled. He had questions, but wanted to hear her answers first somehow. "I gather that because I'm supposed to be your brother, it's assumed I'll go along with whatever's going on here?"

"That's right," she said, smoothing the apron with her hands, then sitting down opposite him. She poured more coffee into the blue-willow cup, then set the electric percolator down on the table top on a large trivet. "I called work—told them I'd be in late. They understood, with my brother coming to town and all."

Rourke forked the last piece of steak, then looked at the woman across from him. "Telephones?"

"Um-hmm." She nodded, smiling.

He looked on the table at the folded newspaper. "May I?"

"We're probably the only town this size in America with a daily newspaper," she said with a definite air of pride, handing it to him.

He opened the paper. The headline read: HALLOWEEN FESTIVITIES SET FOR TONIGHT. A heading on a column read: SCHOOL BOARD ELECTION RESULTS TALLIED.

"School board election?"

"Day before yesterday." She smiled.

"And yesterday was the Fourth of July."

"Um-hmm." She nodded, fingering back a wisp of dark hair with a touch of gray in it.

"And tonight's Halloween?"

"For the children—they love it so." She smiled.

"Tomorrow night Thanksgiving?"

"Yes."

Rourke sipped at his coffee; she had drunk from the same pot so he trusted it. He trusted nothing else in the town.

Chapter 19

Sarah Rourke put a fresh piece of wood into the free-standing stove; it had been converted from propane, she guessed. There were plenty of chairs and table legs remaining and the weather seemed to be moderating slightly. She stood up, letting the children continue to sleep in the bed. She had thrown the bodies overboard, and all of the bedding. Because of the fresh air, the mattress hadn't taken on the smell of the bodies, of the dead man and woman. They had worn wedding rings, and Sarah assumed they had been husband and wife.

The ice had melted sufficiently on the deck of the houseboat, and she could walk there—with care. She leaned against the rope railing; the ice there had completely melted and the rope was wet beneath her fingertips. She stared out onto the lake, wondering what horrors lay ahead on the shore.

After disposing of the bodies, she had gotten the houseboat belayed to a large tree trunk growing near enough to the water, then she'd brought Michael and Annie down the rise with the horses. She had used Tildie and Sam as draft animals to tow the houseboat along the water's edge, toward a better and more even piece of shoreline and to a jetty nearby. There children and animals had boarded. The animals were now tethered in

119

the center of the main room of the houseboat—the carpet destroyed and the animals cramped, but warmer. Then with Michael and Annie, she had rigged an anchor from a heavy deadfall tree the horses had towed down. She had planned to pole the boat away from the shoreline if possible and had been in the process of searching for something with which to do the poling when Annie had pressed a switch on the engine controls—the engines had rumbled to life for an instant. Sarah had dried off the battery terminals, then started the engines again; this time the engines caught. Twin inboards, she had determined, and the fuel gauges read over half full. She had used the engine power to bring them to the center of the lake, and had dropped the anchor there for a safe night—the first she had spent in—

She lurched forward, against the railing, hearing a tearing sound, the breaking of wood, the straining of metal. Behind her, the anchor rope had broken. She stared dumbly at where it had been, then down at the water. There was a current. There hadn't been a current.

She ran into the main cabin. Finding her saddlebags and snatching the binoculars from them, she ran back on deck and focused the binoculars toward the dam at the far end of the lake.

"Jesus!! No!" She screamed the words. The dam had burst. The deck under her rocked; the horses inside the cabin whinnied, screaming, too, if animals could scream.

Annie's voice rang out to her. "Mommie!"

The houseboat, the warmth, the safety, the possibility of transportation it had offered, was being swept toward the dam in a rapidly increasing current.

Sarah Rourke stared skyward a moment at the gray clouds moving on a stiffening wind. She shouted, "Enough, God—enough!"

Chapter 20

Rourke reached down and picked up a can of peaches. It was one of six cans left on the grocery-store shelf, the cans pushed forward, the empty portion of the shelf to the rear and out of casual sight. He was beginning to understand. The peaches, the cereal boxes—even the gasoline he had purchased for the Harley—all "pushed to the front."

As they walked outside—Martha had purchased a can of coffee inside—Rourke said to her, "I think I see it. Leave everything perfectly normal as long as possible, and then—"

"That'll take care of itself." She smiled. "Walk me to the library."

"All right," he nodded. He glanced at his wrist watch as they walked. Seeing children strolling down the street with books in packs on their backs or stuffed under their arms, he thought of Michael and Annie. She would have been— It was three-fifteen in the afternoon. "School's out for today?"

"Yes." She smiled, saying nothing more.

Rourke kept walking with her, in silence, his leather jacket warm to him, but necessary to hide the shoulder rig with the twin Detonics .45s. His Harley was relocked in the garage, his other weapons with it except for the Black Chrome Sting IA which was in its sheath inside the waistband of his Levi's on his left side.

"You don't need your guns," she said, as if she'd been reading his mind. "No one would hurt you. You're my brother."

"But I'm not your brother," he murmured, leaning down to her, smiling, as a group of children passed and waved, calling her "Mrs. Bogen."

"But that doesn't matter." Martha Bogen smiled, then looked at the children. "Hey Tommy, Bobby, Ellen— hey." And she kept walking.

Rourke stopped before they reached the library—the post office down the street from it. An American flag flew from the staff in front of it; a small garden was planted at the base of the staff.

"That's a pretty sight, isn't it—John?" She smiled.

"Yes," Rourke said. It was all he could say.

He felt something bump against him and looked down. A little child, a black mask covering the upper portion of his face, a white straw cowboy hat partially covering carrot red hair. "Sorry, mister," the little boy called out, running past him.

A woman, perhaps twenty-five, was walking after the little boy. She nodded to Martha Bogen and called after the child, "Harry—you take that mask off until tonight. You can't see where you're going!"

Rourke looked after the little boy, saying absently, "I grew up on that guy, him and his friend. Listened to him on the radio, then television."

Martha Bogen said, "Remember—it's Halloween."

"Halloween," Rourke repeated. "Right."

122

He followed her inside the library. As he had by now expected, there were teen-agers in the library, working on reports, it appeared; volumes of encyclopedias and other reference books were spread messily on several of the library tables. An older woman, white-haired, worked at the card catalog.

It was a library—perfectly normal.

"I have a few things to do. If you want you might like to look through the newspaper files," she offered, stopping beside a glass-fronted office.

"What—and read about Memorial Day and Valentine's Day?"

"I'll only be a little bit—I'll get some coffee going, then answer all of your questions."

"I have to leave—very soon," Rourke told her. "And you promised those trails."

"The library closes at five—there'll be plenty of light," she told him, then turned away and started into her office.

Shaking his head, he scanned the library shelves; his eyes stopped on a book that was appropriate—at least part of the title. *War and Peace*. He smiled, murmuring half to himself, "We've had the war part." The white-haired woman at the card catalog looked at him strangely, and Rourke only smiled at her.

At five o'clock, trails or not, he was leaving the town. And if it meant shooting his way past policemen to do it, then he would. If it was Halloween here, he didn't want to find out what the locals meant by trick or treat.

Chapter 21

"Hurry, Michael . . . Annie," Sarah shouted, taking the saddlebags off the back of Tildie's saddle and slinging them over her own shoulder—it could have been a death weight on her, she realized. She ripped a thong from the saddle and lashed the bags that were across her left shoulder under her right arm.

"Michael—you take that knife of yours—and when I tell you to, cut the rope on the railings—hurry."

"All right, Momma," the boy answered, reaching under his coat and producing what looked like a Bowie knife.

"My God—what a thing," she exclaimed. Then she turned to Annie. "You stay with me—take whatever I tell you to carry and do what I say."

The twin inboard engines weren't able to resist the current—she had tried longer than she should have and now it was impossible even to make way for one of the shorelines. But by swimming they might still escape the houseboat before it crashed against the remainder of the high concrete hydroelectric dam—or crashed through the massive gap in the center, to be crushed there where the water spilled now. Either way meant certain death for herself and the children.

But the horses would be strong swimmers, and if they held to the horses there would be a chance to escape the current.

Sarah released Tildie and Sam, then swung up onto Tildie's saddle, reaching down for Annie. "You hold these blankets—don't let go unless you have to or I tell you to." If they made it out alive at all, the water would so soak them that the still-cool air temperatures would bring about chills, perhaps pneumonia. The blankets could be dried over a fire. Annie was in front of her, the little girl's crotch crushed against the front of the saddle.

In her right hand, the arm around Annie, Sarah held Tildie's repaired reins, then in her left she snatched Sam's. She ducked, keeping her head low to avoid crashing it against the ceiling. The houseboat shifted wildly under her now. "Michael—when I shout for you to do it, cut all the ropes you can, then swing aboard Sam and hold on tight and stay with me." She had thought, fleetingly, about tying the children aboard one of the horses, but if the horse were to get in trouble, the children would be powerless to help themselves. She swam, not well, but well enough, Sarah hoped. Annie could paddle around, but it wasn't really swimming. Michael was a strong swimmer for his age and size and could stay afloat—she prayed.

She kneed her horse ahead, holding back tight on the reins for control. Ducking her head but not soon enough, she hit her forehead on the doorframe as Tildie passed through and onto the deck. The boards there were awash with cold spray from the current as the houseboat plowed through the water toward—the dam. She could see it clearly, the gaping holes, as if dynamite had opened it—

or perhaps some crack during the Night of the War, from the bombing. She didn't know what had caused it.

"Michael—the ropes! Cut the ropes. Hurry!"

"Right, Momma." And the boy—not a boy at all she again realized—turned to the ropes, hacking at them.

"Saw with it, Michael—saw with it!"

The boy had the highest of the ropes cut, then began working on the next. Sarah reined in Tildie; Sam, inside the cabin still, bucked and reared. Sarah was hardly able to keep the reins in her hands. "Hurry, Michael! Hurry! I can't hold the horses much longer!" The second rope was cut. The boy glanced toward her once, then ignored her advice, and took the heavy-bladed Bowie pattern knife and chopped with it against the lower and final rope— again and again, the knife blade bounced up toward his face. "Michael!" she screamed, but the last rope was cut.

She knew now that she could never get him aboard Sam. She edged Tildie forward, as Michael sheathed the knife. "Climb up behind me—and don't you let go of me," she heard herself shriek. Michael tugged at her left arm as she loosed Sam's reins, her arm aching as she helped him swing up behind her.

"Hold on!" she shouted, digging her heels into the frightened mare under her. The horse jumped ahead, through the opening in the guardrail and into the water. The mare's head went down, then surfaced. Sarah was washed in a wave of ice-cold spray that made her shiver. Annie screamed; Michael said, "I've got you, Momma!"

Sarah Rourke glanced behind her once. Sam had jumped for it, but she lost sight of him in the next instant. Now the houseboat was swirling toward the opening in the dam, spinning wildly like a leaf in a whirlpool.

"Tildie—save us, Tildie," Sarah shouted, afraid to dig

in her heels, the horse floundering under her. "Tildie!"
she cried, as the horse's head went down.

"We've gotta jump, Momma," Michael shouted to her.

Sarah bit her lower lip, thought she had screamed;
then, holding Annie tight in her arms, she shouted above
the roar of the waters around her, "Michael—don't let go
of me. And if I go under, you save Annie—do it." She
jumped, her left foot momentarily caught up in the
stirrup, then free as Tildie washed away in the current.

"Tildie," she shouted, the animal gone from sight.
Michael clung to Sarah's neck. Sarah wanted to tell him
to loosen his grip; it choked her, but she was afraid she'd
lose him.

The saddlebags were filled with water now; the AR-15
was lost, their food and clothing gone except for what
little she had in the bags.

She was swimming, fighting the current. Annie's
mouth dipped under the water; Sarah fought to keep her
up. Her breath, her own strength, was failing her; then
Michael was gone.

"Michael!"

"Here," he shouted, suddenly beside her, no longer
behind her, holding her left arm, helping her support his
sister. "Momma—there's the shore!"

Sarah looked up, the water pelting her face like waves
of solid substance, slapping at her, hurting her.

She could see it—the shoreline, a muddy bank. She
reached out her right arm, almost losing Annie, catching
at the girl, the little girl saying, "I'm frightened,
Mommie!"

"I am, too," Sarah cried as she saw the shoreline move
rapidly away from her. Glancing to her right, she saw the
opening in the dam growing wider by the instant. The

houseboat was now batting against the sides of the dam, then suddenly was sucked through, lost.

She reached out her right arm again; Michael was trying to tow her. She wanted to tell him to save himself—so at least one of them would survive.

"Michael!"

"Keep going. Come on, Momma!" he shouted, water splashing across his open mouth, making him cough. Sarah was reaching, pulling, tugging, reaching, pulling, the shoreline still speeding past as she was pulled down by the current; but the shoreline somehow looked closer.

Michael was pulling at her, pulling at Annie—she couldn't understand what drove him.

She kept moving her arms, not really conscious of them anymore, not knowing if it was doing any good.

Left arm, right arm, left arm . . . She wanted to sleep, to open her mouth to the water.

She kept moving, her legs too tired now to push her.

Something hard, harder than the water hit at her face and she looked up—red clay, wet and slimy and . . . she wanted to kiss it.

Her left arm reached out, then her right, dragging Annie. The little girl was coughing, almost choking. Sarah slapped her on the back. "Annie!"

Annie slumped forward into the muddy clay and rolled onto her back, crying—alive.

"Michael!"

He wasn't there—he wasn't—"Michael!" She screamed, coughing, getting to her knees, slipping in the mud. She saw a dark spot on the water, staring into it.

His hair—dark brown, like his father's. "Michael!!" she screamed, tears rolling down her cheeks. Jump in and save him—yes, she thought. But if she died—Annie?

"Mich—" His head went below the surface and she died, but it was up again and his arms waved above the surface and he was coming toward her.

Sarah waded out into the water which thrashed around her waist. She tugged at the thong holding the saddlebags to her, loosed it awkwardly, then hurtled the bags to the shore, shouting to Annie, "Stay there, Annie!"

"Is Michael alive?"

Michael reached toward her and Sarah snatched at his hand. The boy came into her arms, both of them falling; then Sarah pushed them up toward the shore. Michael coughed.

"He's alive, Annie," Sarah whispered.

Michael hugged her, coughing still, and then Annie's arms were around her neck and the little girl was laughing and Sarah was laughing too. She whispered, "Thank God for the Y.M.C.A. pool!"

Chapter 22

Rourke sat sipping the coffee.

"So when the war broke out—well we were always pretty cut off from the outside world, but we knew about it. The television reception here was never very good, but we lost the television stations, then the radio stations we could get. We knew ... all of it, as it happened. We sat up through the night in the town square, most of us, and we could see the lights on the horizons around the valley. We knew what was happening. We all sort of decided that living in a world that had been destroyed wouldn't be living at all. All but six families—and they left. They're probably dead now. See, we don't raise much more than what we have in truck gardens. The gas stations had just gotten their supplies before the war took place, and with no one going anywhere, well, we didn't use much gas. A lot of us—mostly everybody—just walk to work and such."

"So you decided to keep things going—just like before," Rourke told her.

"More or less." She smiled, sipping at her coffee, then pouring fresh coffee for Rourke. "At least to try."

"But—"

"But we realized it couldn't last forever. We only had so much. So we worked it out carefully—all of us. We all did. We were always close-knit—"

"You're not from here," Rourke said flatly, sipping his coffee.

"No. I'm not. It was my husband who was born here. He went away to medical school. We married and he brought me back here with him."

"How did the town live?" Rourke asked her. "I saw that factory—"

"That's only been here the last seven years. It was all cottage industry before that. The factory makes some sort of equipment for the space program or the defense department; the people who work there never were quite sure."

"It doesn't make anything, anymore," Rourke said soberly.

"The factory is still running—"

"Making what?" Rourke heard himself snap.

"What they did before—everything is like it was before."

"That's useless. That's insane! For what purpose?" Rourke asked her. "I mean—O.K., the holiday thing is pretty obvious. Make everyone happy as long as you can—but then what? What'll you do when the food runs out and—"

"We won't do anything."

Rourke lit one of his small, dark tobacco cigars—he was running low on those and would have to restock at the Retreat. "What was your cottage industry?"

"Fireworks." She smiled.

He felt strange—perhaps at the realization of what she was telling him. "You're not—"

131

"When strangers came in after the Night of the War, we asked them to stay. Some of them decided to join us. The rest of them are being taken care of—and they'll be released. That's why the police have gone to twelve-hour shifts."

"When'll they be released?"

"Christmas was always our favorite holiday here, the reunion of family and friends. It's—"

Rourke hammered his hands palm downward onto her desk, then glanced over his shoulder toward the library behind him through the glass partition; it was dark, empty. He looked at his watch. It was after five. His vision was blurring.

"I wanted you to stay."

Rourke stood up, suddenly feeling strange, lurching half across the desk.

"Coffee," he murmured.

"We have the entire valley mined with explosives. And the night after tomorrow night, there'll be a fireworks display and then all of us . . . we'll—"

Rourke fell across the desk, cursing his stupidity. He looked up at her. "Mass—"

"Suicide." She smiled, finishing his thought. "All two thousand three hundred forty-eight people in the town. That's why no one minded the lie, John. When I called you Abe." Rourke was having trouble hearing her, seeing her. He snatched for one of his Detonics pistols, but she held his wrist and he could not move his arm. "I was the only one who didn't have a family. My husband is dead. We had no children—there wasn't ever the time—the time to have children. But now I won't die alone, John."

He started to talk, his tongue feeling thick, unresponsive.

"I helped my husband in the clinic. I know how to use his drugs. You won't be able to do a thing, John—until it's too late, and then you can die with me, John."

She was stroking his head, smiling, and he felt her bend over to him and kiss his cheek. "It'll be all right, John; this is the better way. We'll all die and it will always be the same—normal, like it used to be."

Rourke tried to move his mouth to speak; he couldn't.

Chapter 23

It was heavy rain now, cold but not freezing, dripping down inside the collar of his permanently borrowed Army field jacket, his hair too wet to bother with pulling up the hood. His gloves were sodden. The Schmeisser was wrapped in a ground cloth and the Browning High Power was under his jacket. His boots were wet, the Harley having splashed through inches-deep puddles in the road surface, and the going was slow to avoid a big splash that could drown the engine.

He squinted through his rain-smeared glasses—Kentucky. He was entering Kentucky.

Paul Rubenstein wondered two things: would he ever see Natalia again now that she was safe with Russian troops, and had Rourke made it through the storm to find Sarah and the children yet?

Natalia had told the Russian commander that he, Rubenstein, was a Soviet spy who had been escorting her through American territory because he posed as one and was known to the Resistance people operating the area, thought to be one of them. His stomach churning as he'd done it, Rubenstein had agreed, backed up her story. Natalia's credentials checked; he had been released.

They had shaken hands only, but she had blown him a kiss by pursing her lips as they had spoken a few yards from the Soviet troops. Then he had boarded his machine and started back into the storm.

He had looked at her over his shoulder once; she hadn't waved, but he'd felt she would have if she could have.

And John—that Rourke had gotten through the storm at all wasn't something over which Rubenstein worried—Rourke was all but invincible, unstoppable. But, as he released the handlebar a moment to push his glasses up from the bridge of his nose, Rubenstein wondered—had John Rourke found them yet?

Chapter 24

Tildie had wandered ashore minutes after Sarah had taken Michael out of the water; Annie had been the first to spot her. The animal was visibly shuddering.

Sarah had built a fire by the shoreline in the shelter of some rocks and a red clay embankment; then having done what she could to warm the children, she had mounted Tildie—feeling the only way to warm the animal was to exercise her, then rub her down. Promising to keep them in sight, Sarah had started along the water's edge perhaps twenty feet above the shoreline, the wind of the slipstream around her and the animal, chilling her to the bone, but the animal responding.

Sarah clutched the patched-together reins, leaning into Tildie's mane to let the animal break the wind for her. The air temperature was cold, but vastly warmer than it had been. In her heart, she knew the reason why she rode—to think; and she had another reason as well, to search for Sam, her husband's horse, her son's horse. Tildie couldn't carry Michael, Annie, and herself for very long.

And there was affection as well, the affection between human and animal; she wanted to know that Sam was alive or dead, not half-broken and crushed and suffering.

She reined in Tildie, about a quarter-mile closer to the dam now. On the red clay embankment beneath her she could see a shape, stained with mud, moving in the tree line.

"Sam!" Sarah wasn't ready to risk the embankment with Tildie. She dismounted, securing Tildie's reins to a sapling Georgia pine, then started down the muddy embankment toward the trees by the shore. She could see the form clearly now—an animal.

She broke through the tree line, stopping. "Sam!"

The horse, its white hide covered in a wash of red—blood?—started toward her. Closer now, she could see it was only mud. She held out her hands. The animal, frightened and weary, came toward her, nuzzling against her outstretched hands.

"Sam!" She hugged the animal to her, the wetness of her own clothing seeming to wash away some of the red clay mud on the animal's neck. She checked the saddle, that it was secure, then swung up, catching up the rein almost as an afterthought. Her feet dangled below the stirrups which had been set to Michael's leg length.

"Gotta get you out of here, Sam," she cooed, stroking his once-black mane and his red-smeared white neck. "Gotta get out of here." She nudged the animal forward with her knees. . . .

It had taken time to find a way up the embankment, one that the exhausted animal under her could navigate; then she had gone back for Tildie. Sarah had switched to Tildie's back and led Sam, his cinch loosened and some of the mud covering him already flaking away.

By the time she returned to the children, Annie was

137

shivering uncontrollably and Michael was gone. Her heart seemed to stop, but then Michael reappeared, more wood for the fire cradled in his arms. She suddenly noticed he had no jacket—he had given it to Annie.

She warmed Annie with her own body until the shivering subsided to where the little girl could control it. She talked, not to Annie or Michael, not really to herself, but just to think. "I lost my rifle. The horses are exhausted. Those maniacs, the one with the human-teeth necklace and the others, are probably still out there."

She heard something which at once frightened her and comforted her. It would be Brigands; but the sound was that of a truck engine. . . .

She left Michael with Annie and the horses, a half mile away, and hid herself, shivering in her wet clothes, in a bracken of pines not far from the water's edge. There was one truck, a pickup, and in the back of it, she noticed cans of extra fuel. With extra gasoline, she could run the truck's heater. It was a Ford, and she had driven Ford pickups often. She could drive this one.

There were ten Brigands in sight, and if two rode the pickup truck it matched with the number of motor-cycles—eight bikes in all. Holding her husband's .45 automatic in her right fist she wiped the palm of her hand against the thigh of her wet jeans. She did not know whether gunpowder was destroyed by water; would the gun shoot at all, would it blow up on her? There was only one way to find out.

She started down from the trees, edging closer toward the shore. The Brigands huddled by a fireside away from the vehicles, their weapons on the ground beside them or leaning beside tree trunks. She recognized some of the guns as Colt-type rifles, perhaps AR-15s like the gun she had lost in the lake.

All would be lost if the key had been removed from the truck. She knew cars and trucks could be started without keys, but she didn't know how. Her track shoes squishing, the bandanna wet over her hair, her body shivering under the woolen coat, she edged toward the front of the truck. She ducked, hiding by the grill, listening as one of the Brigands rasped, "I gotta take a leak—be back in a second."

She heard gravel crunching—louder, coming toward her.

She pressed her body against the front of the truck; the engine was still warm and she could feel its heat. The gravel crunching and the sound of the Brigand's feet against the dirt were coming closer, becoming louder.

The .45, cocked with the safety off, was in her right hand. She held her breath.

The man passed her, walking off into the trees from which she had come.

She let out a long sigh, then upped the safety on her pistol and peered around behind the rear of the truck, toward the other Brigands.

They still huddled around the fire—nine of them. She pushed herself up to her full height and came around toward the driver's side. The button on the door was up. Before touching the door, she looked inside. "Thank you, God," she murmured. The keys were in the ignition.

She shifted the pistol to her left hand, then with her right hand tried the door handle. It opened easily, the door creaking slightly on its hinges. She waited. None of the Brigands turned around.

She started up into the truck, then heard, "Hey—

hey, bitch!"

She glanced behind her, toward the front of the truck. It was the man who'd passed her, gone into the trees to urinate. In that instant, she cursed men for being able to do it so fast.

Sarah Rourke shifted the gun into her right hand, worked down the safety with her right thumb and pointed the pistol straight out between the open door and the body of the truck. She didn't say, "Hold it—don't come any closer." An old Sarah Rourke would have said that. She felt it in her bones. She pulled the trigger, the pistol bucking once in her right hand; the man's face exploded in blood.

She dismissed him mentally, climbing aboard and setting down the pistol, the safety upped again. Her right hand worked the ignition, her left foot the clutch, her right foot the gas. She hadn't driven in so long, she thought. The engine rumbled reassuringly, then caught.

With her left elbow, she pushed down the door-lock button to give herself an extra instant while she found the emergency brake.

She heard the creaking of hinges, looked across the seat, and saw a face—one of the Brigands. "What the fu—" She picked up the pistol as the man started for his, and she fired. His left eye seemed to explode and the body slumped away.

She found the emergency brake, released it, and popped the clutch, looking to her left; there was a man clinging to the driver's side of the truck. She kept driving, hearing the man's muted curses, the hammering of his fist against the window.

Looking behind her, seeing the angry eyes of the man who held on, Sarah worked the transmission into reverse. She accelerated, the rear end of the Ford smashing into the motorcycles, her body lurching as she stomped on the brakes. She forgot the clutch; the engine died. The man still hung on, hammering against the window. She depressed the clutch with her left foot, working the key again. The engine wasn't catching. She could hear gunfire, shots pinging against the hood of the truck. She sucked in her breath, almost screaming; there was a smashing sound, of glass. She saw what the bullet had hit—the right-hand outside mirror was gone.

She tried the key again, murmuring, "Please—start—please!"

The engine rumbled to life and she put the stick into first; then as she started downward pressure on the gas, she popped the clutch, the truck lurching ahead under her. She glanced into the rear-view—the bikes were a mass of twisted metal behind her, jammed into the trees like paper clips into a box.

The man clinging beside her was still hammering on the glass. Another of the Brigands threw himself toward the hood. Sarah cut the wheel hard right, and the man slid away.

There was more gunfire, the window behind her head spider-webbing with a bullet hole, but not shattering.

She kept driving, the man behind her hammering on the glass with his head now, screaming at her. She had to get away. A stray bullet could hit the gasoline in the back of the truck, could kill her—and what would happen to Michael and Annie.

She couldn't roll down the window to shoot the man. Instead, she sideswiped the Ford into the trees, and the man screamed so loudly she could hear it distinctly.

There was red blood smeared against the driver's-side

141

window now as she upshifted and started away; men, visible in the outside mirror on the driver's side, were running behind her, firing. But she didn't think they would catch her.

After leading the Brigands off, she returned for Michael and Annie. Then she checked the gasoline. It would be enough to get them to Tennessee, to the Mulliner farm, or close enough at least, she judged.

The children, for the last ten minutes, had been wrapped in the blankets found in the back of the truck. They were sitting in the truck cab, naked under the blankets, the heat running full.

She picked up Sam's saddle and tossed it inside the truck bed, then did the same with Tildie's saddle.

She walked over to the animals, hugged Tildie at the neck, and stroked Sam's forehead between the dark eyes. "I love you guys," she whispered, kissing Tildie's muzzle, then slipping her bridle. She slipped Sam's bridle, then swatted both horses on the rumps, sending them off along the shoreline. She looked after them for an instant, manes cutting the wind, tails high. She turned away and cried.

Chapter 25

The air felt almost warm to her. The wind lashed back her hair as the borrowed motorcycle rumbled between her legs, her body leaning into it as she navigated a tight turn, and read a sign, water-stained and half knocked down. There had been a museum there; it was now a barracks. Natalia gunned the Kawasaki ahead. The response didn't seem like that of Rourke's bike. Rourke, she thought.

She wondered if he had found them yet. Were they back in the Retreat, picking up their lives together? And Paul—she smiled. He was a good man, a good friend to them both.

"Both," she repeated into the wind, not hearing it because of the slipstream. Words like both, or us—they were meaningless to her now.

The shore of Lake Michigan seemed remarkably peaceful to her—she watched the smallish whitecaps far off beyond the parkways, liking her view, but sorry for it. She squinted her eyes tight shut, then opened them, realizing how tired she was. She had not wanted to stay with the Soviet troops who had found her with Paul. She had driven with them toward Gary, Indiana, then borrowed the motorcycle, taking something called "Skyway" and winding her way toward South Lake Shore Drive through what remained of Chicago. The buildings stood, but not a tree grew, not a blade of grass; not a dog yelped in the streets. There were no children. The neutron bombing had seen to that.

She followed the drive north, toward the museum that Varakov so religiously preserved, despite the fact that her uncle used it as his headquarters. And the KGB headquarters were there as well. She wondered, almost absently, if Rozhdestvenskiy had arrived yet from the Soviet Union, to replace her late husband. There had been rumors that he had, and unconfirmed though they had been, she hadn't doubted them.

She almost missed the turnoff, left into the small drive past the museum; not bothering to stop, she slowed so the guards could identify her.

She made a left onto the southbound drive, then a fast left into the museum parking lot, past more guards. The guards saluted, Natalia only nodding.

She parked the bike at the foot of the museum steps, dismounting as she let down the stand. She ran her hands across her face, through her hair.

"Major Tiemerovna . . . you are—"

"Alive." She smiled, looking at the face that belonged to the voice. It was that of a young corporal, a frequent sentry at the museum. "Thank you for caring." She smiled again. "Please, make arrangements to return this motorcycle to Captain Konstantin with the forces in Gary, Indiana; it was a loan."

"Yes, Comrade Major." The younger man saluted. She nodded, gesturing toward her clothes, then started up the steps, two at a time, the pistols shaking in the holsters against her hips; the gun barrels with the American Eagles on them had elicited raised eyebrows on her comrades in Indiana. She smiled thinking about that. A gift given in friendship—she would **use** them from now on.

She stopped at the height of the steps to look at the sun, appearing reddish orange over the lake.

How long would from now on be? she wondered. She thought of Rourke, and she shook her head, tossing her hair back as she moved through the brass-looking doors into the museum; then she started across the vast main hall. She saw the figures of the mastodons that her uncle seemed so obsessed with watching, studying. And beyond them, on the small mezzanine, where she had thought she would find him, he stood, staring—at the mastodons.

There were men and women moving about the main hall, office workers, messengers. Ignoring them, she shouted, running now, past the mastodons, "Uncle Ishmael!"

The face turned toward her as she called again "Uncle!" She saw his thick lips forming into a smile, his arms outstretching, his uniform blouse opening. And as his arms expanded toward her and she took the mezzanine steps two at a time, running, his jacket opened wider, revealing the potbelly he had always had ever since her first remembrance of him—like a father. And like a daughter, she came into his arms, hugging his neck, feeling the strength of his arms around her.

"Natalia Anastasia," he murmured.

"Uncle." And she held him tightly.

"You are well, child?" he asked, folding her in his right arm, turning to stare across the museum's great hall.

She stood beside him. "Yes, Uncle—I am well."

"The storm—when I heard that our troops found you, my heart—if an old man's heart can sing, then mine did," he said, not looking at her.

She studied his face.

"When I did not receive word from Chambers, the American president, I was frightened. For you."

"John Rourke flew all of us out of Florida, Uncle; he helped Paul Rubenstein find his parents. We took off just as—"

"Just as the final tremor hit. Thank—" He looked at her and laughed. "Yes, thank Lenin's ghost, child." And he laughed again. "That man, the mole agent who accompanied you when our troops found you, I assume he was Paul Rubenstein, the young Jew?"

"Yes, Uncle," she answered, her voice low, looking away. "I couldn't—"

"Betray a friend? I would not have expected you to, child. But I need to know. It is important. Is it the young—"

"Yes. It was Paul Rubenstein," she told him, fishing in her bag for her cigarettes, finding one, then a lighter, working the lighter, and then inhaling the smoke deep into her lungs.

"Such a bad habit—this smoking. You do it more since the death of Karamatsov."

"I know." She smiled, exhaling the smoke through her nostrils, watching it hang on the air for a moment, then begin to dissipate.

"You may see Rourke again—soon. Does this distress you?"

"He's been captur—"

"Captured? Hardly. I think he is more ghost than man, sometimes. No. But I must speak with this man of yours."

She felt her hand trembling as she touched the end of the cigarette to her lips, inhaling the smoke. "He is not—"

"The wrong phrase, then." Varakov smiled. "Can you find Rourke for me?"

"Uncle, I—"

"I would not ask if it were not of vital importance. I need someone who has honor, someone who—I will explain it all to you later, Natalia. You cannot find him?"

"I do not know where to look, Uncle," she answered. "The storm—he went into it, to search for his wife and children—"

"Alone. And he sent this Rubenstein with you, to care for you?"

"Yes. I tried to tell him I could—"

"It matters little, child, to a man who loves a woman, that she can care for herself, perhaps better under some circumstances than he could care for her, or have her cared for. He did what I would have done. He has two lives, and is loyal to them both. He pursued one while he sent the other of his two lives under the care of this man who seems to be his best friend. He should be Russian, this Rourke."

"I wish he were." She smiled, then looked away.

Her uncle, Natalia not looking at him as he spoke, said, "You will give me as complete a description as possible of Rubenstein, of the vehicle he drove—"

"A motorcycle—like Rourke's, only blue."

"A motorcycle—only blue, yes. And the direction in which he would be traveling. Even now Rozhdestvenskiy is rerouting my retreating troops, forming a strike force. I must talk with this Rubenstein in order to find Rourke. He has a place where he operates from—and this Jew can find it for me. I must talk with Rourke."

"Why?" She looked at her uncle then.

"You must trust me—that Rubenstein will not be harmed, nor will Rourke. And while my men search for this young man, I have a job for you. It is perhaps the most dangerous mission you have ever had."

"Where must I go, Uncle?"

"Into Rozhdestvenskiy's private office. Walk with me and we shall discuss it."

Her palms sweated as she stubbed out the cigarette in a pedestal ashtray, then followed him slowly—because his feet hurt, she could tell—down the steps.

Chapter 26

As he leaned back in his chair, the telephone cradled beside his left ear, against his shoulder, Nehemiah Rozhdestvenskiy studied his face in the reflection of the mirror opposite his desk. He studied the toes of his shoes; they sparkled.

"Yes," he answered into the receiver. "Yes, Comrade. . . . I cannot hear you. . . . The connection is . . . yes—now. Work goes ahead on the Womb construction. . . . I have already begun martialing forces to restart the factories needed. . . . No, Comrade, I have not made copies of the Eden Project documents. Should they fall into the wrong hands . . ." He coughed, covering up, he hoped, the fact that he had been about to interrupt Anatol Tporich, the supreme head of the KGB. "No, Comrade. A courier even now brings to your offices a copy of the abstract and my initial report of the findings. There can be no mistake. The factories will work four six-hour shifts to keep the laborers and technicians fresh. They will be housed in the factories and not allowed outside contact. . . . And—" He coughed again, to cover another interruption. "Yes, Comrade—only KGB personnel . . . No, Comrade—not Major Tiemerovna. I agree that her loyalties may lie—" Tporich was lecturing him about security and Rozhdestvenskiy disliked anyone lecturing him on a subject at which he himself was so expert. "I will be constantly vigilant, Comrade. . . . I am losing your voice, Comrade!" There was much static. High-altitude bombers were being used as communications relays for overseas radio transmissions with all satellites down or out of service since the Night of the War. "There . . . I hear you. Yes, Comrade." Rozhdestvenskiy lit a cigarette, studying his gleaming teeth in the mirror for a moment as he did. "Yes. . . . I realize, Comrade, how little time remains. The Womb will be ready. . . . This I swear as a loyal member of the party."

The line clicked off, dead.

Rozhdestvenskiy studied the abstract of the Eden Project again. It was clear, concise, but incomplete. He needed more information. But he had not told Tporich that. He would find out what he needed to know in time. He had to, in order to live.

And to live—he had always felt—was all. After life, there was nothing.

Chapter 27

Rubenstein felt better. He was making better time. The weather was almost warm again as he moved through Kentucky, nearing the Tennessee line, the Harley eating the miles since he had made the stop near the strategic fuel reserve of which Rourke had told him.

There was slush, heavy slush at the higher elevations. And in case the temperature dropped with evening, he wanted to get as far south as possible. If he pressed, he could get near the Georgia line and be well toward Savannah by nightfall. By now, Rourke should be crisscrossing the upper portion of the state and into the Carolinas, looking for Sarah and the children. Perhaps—Rubenstein felt himself smile at the thought—perhaps Rourke had already found them. Should he, Rubenstein, start for the Retreat?

He should follow the plan, he decided. If Rourke had designed it, it was—Rubenstein looked up; a helicopter, American but with a Soviet star stenciled over it, was passing low along the highway, coming up fast behind him.

"Holy shit!" Rubenstein bent low over the machine, running out the Harley to full throttle. He had almost forgotten about the Russians; and what were they doing? "Joy riding," he snapped, releasing the handlebar a moment to push his wire-rimmed glasses back off his nose. "Damn it!"

The helicopter was directly above him, hovering. Rubenstein started to reach for his pistol to fire, but the machine pulled away, vanishing up ahead of him.

Rubenstein braked the Harley, glancing to his right; there was a dirt road, little more than a track. He wondered if he could take it. Should he? The helicopter was coming back, toward him, and Rubenstein had no choice. He wrenched the bike into a hard right, sliding across the slushy highway toward the dirt road beyond, jumping the bike over a broad flat low rock. As his hands worked the controls, the bike came down hard under him, and throttled up to take the incline with some speed as he started up the dirt track.

There was a loudspeaker sounding behind him. "Paul Rubenstein. You are ordered to stop your machine. You are ordered to stop and lay down your arms. You will not be harmed."

Rubenstein glanced skyward, at the helicopter almost directly over him.

He bounced the bright blue Harley up over a ridge of dirt and onto a board bridge. There was a second helicopter now, joining the pursuit.

The loudspeaker again. "You will injure yourself if you pursue this course of action. We mean you no harm." The voice was heavily accented. "You are ordered to surrender!"

"Eat it!" Rubenstein shouted up to the helicopter, the downdraft of the rotor blades making his voice come back to him. Ahead of him he could see the second helicopter, hovering low, too low over the road where it widened. He could see uniformed troopers in the massive open doors of the formerly U.S. machine.

He heard the Russian voice again on the loudspeaker. "Paul Rubenstein. This is by order of General Varakov; you are to stop immediately and lay down your arms."

Rubenstein spotted what Rourke had told him once was a deer trail; it looked the same. He wrenched the bike into a hard left, onto the deer trail, the branches cracking against his face and body as he forced the machine through. The path was bumpier than the dirt road he had just left.

"Paul Rubenstein . . . you are ordered to—"

He looked up, cursing under his breath, then looked ahead of him. A deadfall tree lay across the path. He started to brake, and the Harley skidded from under him. Rubenstein threw himself clear, hitting the ground hard.

He pushed himself to his feet, the Harley lost somewhere in the trees. He started to run, snatching at the battered High Power under his jacket. He stopped at the tree line, snapping off two fast shots toward the nearest helicopter; the machine backed off. He had lost sight of the other one after heading onto the deer path.

Machine-gun fire was coming at him, hammering into the ground and the trees ten yards behind him as he ran, swatting away the tree branches that snapped at his face. Pine boughs still laden with snow pelted him, washing wet snow across his face. The machine-gun fire was edging closer and he dropped to his knees, wheeling, firing the High Power in rapid, two-shot semiautomatic bursts.

The helicopter backed off.

"Son of a gun." He smiled, pushing himself to his feet,

turning to run again.

Three Russian soldiers blocked the path. The other helicopter, he realized, had landed its men.

Rubenstein started to bring the pistol on line to fire, but something hammered at the back of his neck and he fell forward, the gun dropping from his grip.

Hands reached down to him; voices spoke to him in Russian. Rubenstein rolled onto his back, his left foot snapping up and out, into the crotch of one of the Russians; the man doubled over.

Rubenstein reached up, snatching hold of a fistful of uniform, hauling himself up to his knees as he dragged the soldier down, his left fist smashing upward, into the face. Then he was on his feet, running. Someone tackled him; he went down, the ground slapping hard against him.

Another man was on top of him, holding him. Rubenstein snapped his left elbow back, found something hard against it, and heard a moan and what sounded like a curse despite the language barrier.

He pushed himself up, wheeling, his left swinging out, catching the tip of a chin. A man fell back under his blow.

Rubenstein wheeled again. He saw the two bunched-together fists swinging toward him like a baseball bat, felt the pain against the side of his neck, then there was nothing but darkness and a warm feeling.

Chapter 28

John Rourke squinted against the light, his belly aching, a sudden stabbing pain in his left upper arm. The pain was familiar—the arm aching like a bad tooth. He moved that arm, but it wouldn't move well. And when he opened his eyes, his vision was blurred. His other limbs didn't work when he told them to. He fell, feeling something tight around his neck, choking him, feeling hands on his shoulders, moving him.

A voice. "John . . . John. I told you the last time, don't try to stand up. You can't walk; don't you know that by now? Thanksgiving's almost past. I'm sorry I couldn't give you any turkey; you've been throwing up everything I give you. But tomorrow's Christmas and then it'll all be over."

Rourke shook his head, murmuring, "I like turkey—Thanksgi— Christmas?"

"I'll help you onto the cot." Above him a woman's face smiled.

"Strong," he muttered, feeling her hands under his armpits. He wanted to help her, very badly because the floor was cold under him. Naked? His hands—he squinted to look at them. Tied together. So were his ankles. The thing around his neck choked him again.

"I'm sorry, John. That rope around your neck—it got caught on the edge of the cot. I'll fix it." The pressure around his neck subsided.

"Thanks—Martha," he murmured. Martha? Martha Bogen? "Coffee," he shouted, his own voice sounding odd to him, his tongue feeling dry and thick and hot.

"Yes. You asked the same question the last two times I gave you an injection. I drugged the coffee with chloral hydrates—I just had to give you so much of it it made you sick. And I gave myself an apomorphine shot after I drank the first cup. I just threw it up. So it didn't bother me. I just made myself throw up. You are very forgetful, John." The voice cooed, good-naturedly.

"Sor—" Why was he sorry? he wondered. Because he was forgetful? He couldn't remember why he was sorry.

There was another needle plunged into his arm, and the pain was there again.

Why was she giving him two shots? He tried to think—if he could think. The nausea—from the chloral hydrate she had said. But not the shots. "Not the shots," he verbalized.

"It'll be all right, John. I'll give you the antidote and when I do in thirty seconds you'll be just fine—honestly. And then we can hold each other's hands maybe and watch when the fireworks start and the mountains start to crash down on us. We'll die together. Neither one of us will ever be alone again, John." He saw her face; it looked distorted to him, like something seen through a tube with the lighting wrong. She was smiling.

"I still have all my husband's drugs, John, so I can bring you out of this very easily when it's time. Just a day or so, really. You'll just feel like you're very drunk and it won't bother you. It hasn't. And then when I give you the antidote you'll be your old self again."

She kissed him on the cheek; he could feel it. He tried moving his arms, but they wouldn't move.

"Now, John," she said with what sounded like a mother's severity to him. "Even if you should get yourself untied, it won't do you any good. With what I've given you, you can't walk and you can't really think too well. You're locked in the library basement and I've taken your clothes and those guns of yours. I'll be back in a few hours with another set of shots. Maybe we can get some good soup or something into you after it all wears off. But I think if I fed you now, well, you'd just get all sick again."

He felt her kiss his cheek again, and then she disappeared from his line of sight.

He heard a door open, shut, and the sound of a key in a lock.

There was nothing else to do, he thought, so he started to move his shoulders and his hips. He kept moving them, throwing his weight to his right; then he rolled.

The basement floor slapped hard against his body and the side of his face. The pain—it cleared his head. He rolled with much effort, twisting his body and throwing his weight, onto his back. He tried to move his legs; they wouldn't move. He squinted against the light, looking at the ropes on his hands. Ordinary rope—clothesline, he thought. He tried tugging against the rope; his arms didn't respond.

"Muscle relaxant—curare deriv—" He felt the nausea welling up inside him and leaned back his head, staring at

157

the ceiling. He looked behind him, awkwardly. An end of the clothesline snaked across the floor and was tied to a support post for the basement ceiling. When he moved his head, the rope moved a little; it was the rope that had him tethered by the neck.

Muscle relaxant, he thought. If she didn't know how to administer it, he would stop breathing, just die. She was only giving him enough so that it would wear off every few hours.

The swimming feeling in his head—the nausea, the cold . . . The muscle relaxant wouldn't make him, like she had said, "drunk." He closed his eyes a minute against the feelings. . . .

"Mor—" he shouted, the needle jabbing into his arm again. "Morphine!"

"You've had morphine before, then, John, and you recognize the effects. Well, then you know it would take an awful lot to addict you, wouldn't it? And anyway, well—all our problems will be over."

Hours had passed, he realized. What time was it? Was it Christmas? He felt the second needle going in. "I have to go now, John. Please try to stay on the bed this time."

He felt her kiss him again, and then heard the click of her heels on the concrete floor. "Insane!" he shouted, but he realized then that he'd already heard the door opening and closing, the lock being turned.

"Mor—morphine," he said with a thick tongue. Thirty seconds, he thought—something about thirty seconds. He would be himself again in thirty seconds. The muscle relaxant had to wear off well before she gave him the morphine. The muscle relaxant would be something . . . "Morphine," he said again. "Narcan."

Rourke realized suddenly that if she kept it up, she'd kill him. He could barely breathe—which meant there was a build-up and she was giving the shots too closely spaced.

"Die," he rasped. Morphine—he could fight that, with his body. But the relaxant . . . He vomited over the side of the bed and his eyes closed.

Chapter 29

Natalia watched as he closed the door. She had been
formally reintroduced to Rozhdestvenskiy that afternoon, and now things were less than formal. But she did
wear black, a tight-fitting jump suit, a black scarf tied
across her face like a bandanna, a second scarf binding
and covering her hair, black tight-fitting leather gloves
on her hands. She usually used less tight-fitting, fingerless cloth gloves for work like that she was about to per-
form, but the fingerless gloves would have allowed her to
leave behind fingerprints. That she could not do. Were
she discovered raiding the office of the head of the
American branch of KGB, she would be tried and
executed—and so would her uncle. Likely, her uncle's
secretary, Catherine, too, and perhaps, others of her
uncle's staff.

Rozhdestvenskiy walked directly under her, and she
watched his face through the slats in the air-conditioning
vent. She glanced at the Rolex on her left wrist, watching
the minutes pass as she waited to make certain he was
indeed gone.

She had crawled in through the air-conditioning
system on the far end of the floor—through her uncle's

office. She had traveled through the dusty duct for what seemed like miles. Using a needle-thin powerfully magnetized angled screwdriver, she had released the screws holding the vent in place, then waited. No one had come in or out; security was at the far end of the corridor. She knew that routine too well, and decided Rozhdestvenskiy hadn't had the time to change things substantially. It was her dead husband's old office.

She released the little hook that held up the vent, slipping the vent aside and drawing it up into the duct with her. It banged once, slightly, against the duct and she froze as she heard boot heels clicking down the corridor under her. A guard passed, not looking up. She held her breath, waiting.

He walked back, directly under her again, and stopped. She waited, coiled, ready to jump for him. If she were spotted coming out of the vent, if she were spotted at all . . . She waited, and as the guard moved past her, she breathed again.

She continued to move the grill, then set it aside in the duct. She listened, hard, holding her breath. It would have been better to wait for nightfall, to wait for a later hour when the guards would be drowsy from lack of sleep.

She perched on the edge of the duct, then tucked her shoulders tight, letting her feet down and raising her arms as she dropped.

She hit the floor eight feet below, rolled forward into the fall, and came to light on her hands and knees. She pushed herself up, then went flat against the wall. No sound of a guard coming. She had made no sound when she'd left the duct.

She turned, glancing toward Rozhdestvenskiy's office,

then glanced back up the hall. The guards were still where they should be, by the mouth of the corridor.

She started toward Rozhdestvenskiy's door.

She took the key from inside her glove, tried it, and the knob turned under her hand; the door opened. She dropped the backpack from her shoulders, and reached inside one of the outside pouches. She took a small leather pack, about twice as high as a package of cigarettes and half as thick. She opened it and pulled a pick from it. Taking the pick and scratching it against the lock surface, then breaking it against the lock surface, she left the small broken end piece on the floor, then reclosed the pack. She deposited the stem of the pick and the lock-pick set pack in her backpack, then closed the outer compartment and stepped inside the office.

Natalia closed the door behind her, quickly. To the best of her uncle's knowledge and to the best of her intelligence she had not aroused suspicion; no ultrasonic or photoelectric alarm systems had been installed. There would be the pressure-sensitive plates inside his office, but there should be nothing in the outer office. She stepped across the room, in darkness, taking the side chair, which sat next to the secretarial desk, and carrying it back toward the door into the corridor. She opened the door halfway, listening at first; there was no sound. She opened it fully. A quick glance revealed no one in the corridor except the guards at the far end. They were not turning around. Moving rapidly, the chair in both hands, she started into the hallway, positioning the chair under the open duct vent. Pulling a third black scarf, like the two covering her face and hair, from her side pocket, she unfolded it into a square to cover the seat; then stood on it atop the chair seat. The magnetic screwdriver was in

162

her left side pocket and she got it out; then reaching up into the duct, she pulled the cover slightly closer and inserted it over the opening. She started tightening the screws.

Natalia froze at the voice of one of the guards—a remark about hearing something.

She shifted the screwdriver to her left hand to hold in place the screw on which she was working; her right hand reached for the Bali-Song knife in the hip pocket of her jump suit. The knife, unopened, in her right fist, she held her breath, listening.

To kill an innocent Soviet guard was anathema to her—but she would if she had to.

Natalia kept waiting.

There were no footsteps.

Dropping the knife back into her hip pocket, she resumed tightening the screws in the vent cover.

Quietly, she stepped down from the chair, snatching the black silk scarf and stuffing it into her pocket, the screwdriver having already been returned to her other pocket. Then she picked up the chair, which she set down to reopen Rozhdestvenskiy's outer office door. Having brought the chair inside, she replaced it exactly as it had been, that was crucial, she realized.

Natalia crossed the room to Rozhdestvenskiy's inner office door, her pack in her left hand, swinging by the straps. It would not be locked. She opened the door, snatching the Kel-Lite flashlight from her pack, scanning the floor, the walls—if additional alarms had been installed, they were not readily visible.

She closed her eyes, remembering the pattern of the pressure-sensitive plates, the way in which Karamatsov had walked when leaving his office for the night with her.

But it had to be the reverse. He was coming from the desk and the small safe behind it; she was going toward it.

She took a long-strided step to her left, shifted her weight and brought her right foot up, beside it. She waited. It was a silent alarm—but it would bring the guards almost instantly. She took the next step, again to her left, trying mentally to measure and match her dead husband's stride. She brought her right foot over, waiting again.

She was a third of the way across the room.

She took a broad step to the right, losing her balance momentarily, her left foot almost touching the carpet in the wrong spot. She sucked in her breath hard, regaining her balance, waiting, settling her left foot beside the right.

Natalia took another step, then another and another.

She remembered how foolish Vladimir had looked, sitting on his desk, swinging his feet around to avoid the plates flanking his desk on both sides.

Now, she shifted her weight forward, onto her finger-tips, then threw her pack onto the desk top. The Kel-Lite was in the black belt around her waist on which she carried a borrowed pistol. Had she lost one of her own guns, the ones given her by President Chambers, it would have meant instant recognition and arrest.

With the flashlight beam zigzagging at a bizarre angle with the rising and falling of her chest, she leaned toward the desk, throwing her weight forward and pushing herself up, jumping, tucking her knees up.

Natalia was on the desk top.

The safe was behind the desk and a little to the right of it. As she turned, she caught a glimpse of herself in the mirror—all made up for the American Halloween, she thought.

She had to move like a spider now, her pack once more on her back, jumping to avoid the pressure-sensitive plates.

She stood on the desk, judging the distance, inhaled deeply, then jumped.

Her feet landed on the top of the small safe, and for a moment, her balance faltered and she started to fall back. But she caught herself, lurching her body forward, then rising to her full height.

Natalia breathed again.

Dropping to her knees, the flashlight in her right hand, she bent over the safe door, upside down, shining the light on the combination lock. Shifting the light into her left hand, she tried the combination.

The combination, as she had suspected, had been changed.

"Damn it," she muttered in English.

She reached into her pack, extracting the specially sensitive stethoscope there.

Untwisting the tubing, she touched the flat diaphragm chest piece to the safe's escutcheon plate, beside the dial.

The door was slightly recessed into the body wall of the safe. She leaned over slightly more, working the combination to the dial's right, then left, then right again, listening. She heard a minuscule clicking in the locking bolt linkage, then stopped. Her gloved fingers worked the dial left, stopping when through the stethoscope's binaural ear tips she could hear another click.

Now right—listening for the click might be more faint. She heard it, but had passed it.

"Damn," she muttered again. She cleared the dial, then reworked the combination she had already memorized, this time without the earpieces to aid her; she had the numbers now.

She worked the handle, heard the bolt-activating gear rings click; the safe opened under her hand.

Natalia reached inside the safe, to the lower shelf.

The six crates of documents were in the cryptoanalysis room, but Rozhdestvenskiy would have the abstract or a copy of it.

Natalia found more than she had anticipated.

Squatting like an Indian on the top of the opened safe, she fished into her pack for the camera. Shining the Kel-Lite on the documents' faces, working the shutter, she caught bits and pieces of words.

"Eden Project . . . in the event of massive nuclear exchanges between our country and the Soviet Union . . . the ultimate statement of the Western democracies . . . this utilization of the Space Shuttle Fleet . . . manufacturing processes . . ." She flipped the page for the next shot. "In the face of the near total destruction of life on the planet . . ." She felt her heart skip a beat, then realized that it hadn't; she was being emotional. ". . . Bevington, Kentucky, and an as yet undesignated site . . . precursed by bizarre atmospheric changes . . ." The third page of the abstract was merely a list of names—she assumed those who had compiled the reports.

She photographed the next document, a simple road map, the kind once sold in American gasoline stations, of the state of Kentucky, with a small town in the mountains, Bevington, circled in red with an arrow pointed toward it coming from the southeast.

Natalia began photographing the last set of documents; it was Rozhdestvenskiy's report. ". . . findings of

Soviet scientists have been verified and coincided with those of Western scientists . . . raid on Bevington, Kentucky, in the south-central United States . . ." Natalia would have called it more southeastern.

She glanced at her Rolex; she had to hurry. Rozhdestvenskiy might be back at any moment. She photographed the second page without taking note of anything written there, then the third and last page. He was admirably concise in his writing she noted subconsciously. ". . . the construction at the site called the Womb, and the bringing together of strategic materials there, is the only hope for the survival of the Soviet."

She shuddered. Survival of the Soviet?

Was survival of the Soviet equivalent with the survival of mankind? she asked herself, closing her eyes from the glare of the flashlight. A doomsday device?

She prayed not; then felt the corners of her mouth raise in a smile—to whom did a good Communist pray?

Carefully, Natalia Anastasia Tiemerovna replaced the documents exactly as they had been in the safe, then she closed the combination, resetting the dial to the number it had been set to before she had touched it.

Natalia stood up, on the top of the safe, shouldering the pack, her gear secured inside it.

In the darkness, her eyes accustomed enough to it with the flashlight packed away, she jumped to the floor, intentionally landing on one of the pressure-sensitive plates. She ran toward the inner office door, knowing the silent alarm was sounding.

She threw open the door, then ran across the outer office, throwing open the door, turning into the corridor and running toward the panic-locked emergency door.

"Halt!" The guard's voice came in clumsy English.

Gunfire ripped into the wall beside her as she hit the panic lock, the door opening outward into a corridor.

She slammed the steel fire door, hearing slugs impacting against it from the inside.

She reached up, clipping the wires for the alarm there into a bypass with alligator-clipped strands of wire of thinner proportion to suck off the electrical charge. Then, with a wire cutter from the left hip pocket of her jump suit, she clipped the alarm wire.

She replaced the wire cutter after scratching the outside locking panel with it—to make it appear she had used a pick after neutralizing the alarm in order to originally gain access.

More gunfire—the door bulged in the center. She released her weight against the door and ran up a small flight of stairs, hearing the door thrown open behind her, more gunfire, louder now, another command in English. "Halt!"

She turned out of the stairwell into a darkened hall— the Egyptian exhibit.

She remembered strolling through it with her uncle. Now she ran its length—more running feet and shouts behind her, the gunfire ceased.

There was a row of sarcophagi and past it an exhibit depicting the dressing of a pyramid block. "Appropriate," she thought, making an English pun on the word "dressing" in her mind. She slipped behind the exhibit case, into a service closet, closing the door behind her.

In total darkness, she slipped the pack from her back, then began to unzip the jump suit with her right hand, her left hand working free the pistol belt. She tugged the zipper down the rest of the way, then with both hands ripped away the scarves that had covered her face and hair. She kicked off the crepe-soled shoes she had worn, reaching down for them in the dark—she thought she heard the skittering of a mouse or rat across the floor. She pulled the Bali-Song knife from the pocket of her jump suit, holding it closed in her teeth while she smoothed the white slip she had worn under the jump-suit trousers, smoothed it down from where it had bunched around her hips.

She reached into the pack, pulling out her skirt.

She put it around her waist, buttoning it once, then again at the waistline in the front. From the pack, she extracted a pair of black high heels, stepped into them, and stuffed everything into the pack, closing it. She released the straps on the pack, hooking them together to form a single strap. She ran her left hand through her hair, then listened at the door—no sound. She opened it a crack, saw no one in the hall and stepped out of the closet. She realized she had forgotten the gloves, then quickly pulled them off, stuffing them into the backpack converted now into a large black shoulder bag.

She could hear running feet in the hall as she looked down at herself, smoothing the skirt, then reaching up to retie the bow on the collar of the white blouse she'd worn under the jump suit.

She turned, she hoped at the dramatically correct moment, and confronted the guard before he could confront her.

"What is going on, Corporal?"

"Comrade Major Tiemerovna, a man—someone from the Resistance apparently. There was an attempt to break into Comrade Colonel Rozhdestvenskiy's office."

"An attempt?"

"Yes, Comrade Major. The alarm system sounded

before anything could be disturbed—Comrade Colonel Rozhdestvenskiy has himself said this. He was just returning when the intruder was discovered."

"Thank goodness." She smiled. Then she let her smile fade, saying to the guard corporal, "You have your rifle but I am unarmed. Give me your pistol and I will search with you, Comrade."

"Thank you, Comrade Major!" The young man's face beamed.

Chapter 30

"Sleeping," Rourke murmured. That he could think, that he had awakened told him it was nearly time for another dose. He knew now just what that was—a muscle relaxant to keep him immobile and morphine to keep him high, drunk. The combination could kill him. If he could convince her of that . . . His mind worked again, but he felt himself moving like a drunkard as he tried to edge over on the cot. If she stopped administering one or the other, he would have a chance to fight the freshly administered drug and the drugs in his system. She would have an antidote, a muscle-relaxer block of some kind, and probably Narcan or something like it to counteract the morphine build-up.

"Respiratory distress," he murmured.

He felt a smile cross his lips, laughed with it. Alcohol had never made him feel so drunk. Rubenstein hadn't been this drunk that time . . . Where was it? he asked himself mentally.

Natalia had been pretty drunk . . . or had she been? Sarah had never drunk to excess in her life; when she drank even a little, it simply made her sleepy.

"Sarah." He smiled, then remembered. They had

Lamazed for both children, Sarah having used the natural childbirth technique, which was really only erroneously called that. It was controlled childbirth—you controlled it with breathing. But you had to learn the breathing techniques well. His mind was wandering and he couldn't organize his thoughts. "Breathing," he murmured, squinting against the overhead basement light. He could make himself appear to be in respiratory distress by hyperventilating.

He started breathing, panting, blowing, panting—building up the oxygen level in his bloodstream. The oxygen would also serve to fight off the drugs by burning them off, out of his system as he respirated.

Floaters appeared in front of his eyes, a cold wash of nausea swept through him, and again he leaned over the side of the cot and vomited, his head barely able to move.

"John! Are you ill?"

"Breathe," he gasped, panting now more than before despite the fact it was actually starting to make him hyperventilate.

"John—my God. I was afraid of this. You. aren't supposed to— Here." She began massaging his chest, then started to give him mouth-to-mouth resuscitation.

He felt her lips against his, felt the rush of air making him choke. He coughed and felt her rolling his head to the side. He vomited again, but nothing came out.

"I'm going to give you this." She reached into a small black leather case and extracted a hypodermic. "This will block the effect of the muscle relaxant I gave you. It'll take effect almost immediately."

He felt the needle, closing his eyes against it and the pain in his already sore arm. "I'll wait with you before I give you more morphine—once the muscle relaxant is gone—and here." He watched as she raised a hypodermic and squirted out a good third of the contents. "A milder dose this time and you'll just rest."

Rourke closed his eyes—not able to help it. He knew he was drunk. He felt like singing because he was so happy she had bought his act. He twitched once in his sleep, feeling the needle go into his arm again. . . .

Chapter 31

Sarah Rourke shivered, despite the warmth from the truck's heater, despite the fact the children, wrapped in their blankets, were warm now.

She had found an M-16 under the seat; it said M-16 on the side. It looked identical to the rifle she had lost so she now adopted it as her own.

She shivered because of what she was doing. She drove the main roads, passing into Tennessee now, and the main roads could mean Soviet troops or Brigands. She knew that Chattanooga had been neutron-bombed; by now it would be safe to drive near or through.

The ground dropped sharply as she saw Chattanooga for the first time—no smoke from its chimneys, no cars. The road angled sharply left and she cut her speed slightly as she made the curve; the pickup's steering was not the world's best, she had decided.

As she started out of the curve, she glanced across at Michael and Annie. They slept in each other's arms.

She looked back at the road. She sucked in her breath, almost screaming.

A hundred yards ahead, perhaps—judging distance accurately had never been her strong point, she knew—

and the road was flanked on the right by the end of a long-reaching column of trucks and other vehicles, motorcycles parked near them. The men standing near the trucks and motorcycles were Soviet troops.

She glanced at the children. They were asleep and she'd let them stay that way.

She slipped the M-16 under the seat, then pulled her .45 and cocked the hammer, locking up the thumb safety catch, then sliding it under her right thigh. She kept driving, not speeding her pace, not slowing. She noticed the quizzical expressions on the faces of some of the Soviet soldiers who turned toward her as she passed.

One young man waved and she waved back, suddenly glancing in the mirror at her hair. It was greasy-looking from being wet so long. She ran her right hand through it. She kept driving.

She made a mental count of the vehicles—in case she reached the Mulliner farm. She could tell Mary's son and he could pass the information to U.S. Intelligence through the Resistance group he worked with.

"Eighty-one, eight-two, eight-three—" She stomped on the brake pedal, almost forgetting the clutch, not knowing what else to do when six soldiers with rifles stepped in front of her truck. The one who seemed the oldest raised his right hand in a gesture for her to stop.

Her blood froze.

Glancing into the rear-view, she saw, through the bullet-holed window, men closing ranks behind her.

The older man approached her truck on the driver's side.

She rolled down the window.

His English was heavily accented but perfectly understandable to her.

"Your papers—travel permits."

"I—I, ahh—"

"They are lovely children there. I must see your papers, madam."

She glanced at Michael and Annie, still sleeping. "Thank you—my son and daughter."

"Your papers, madam." He smiled, his right hand outstretched.

She could shoot him, she thought—but then, Michael and Annie would be killed when all the others with their rifles and handguns would shoot back.

"I—I don't—"

"What is the problem, Sergeant?"

She looked away from the sergeant's face, in the same direction the sergeant, the older man with the smile, turned and looked.

A tall officer, perhaps in his late thirties. Good-looking. She knew the face.

"Major—" she gasped, feeling like a fool—and feeling trapped.

"Comrade Major Borozeni, I stopped this truck to request papers of this woman. She apparently has no travel permit."

"I, ah—" She started to lie, but saw the look of recognition in the major's eyes—and the eyes, the face, they were all familiar. She had last seen him, hatless, wet, swearing after her in the rain outside of Savannah, after she had held him at gunpoint and forced him to help her effect the release of the Resistance fighters.

"I will handle this, Krasny," the major said. "Take your men aside."

The major approached the truck cab. Standing just a yard or so from the side of the door, his height was such that she knew he could watch her every move—if she went for her gun.

"Sarah, wasn't it?"

"Yes, Major—Sarah," she nodded, feeling somehow more tired than she had ever felt. "You caught me," she said, looking at his face.

"I think about you—a great deal. They are lovely children. They are yours?"

"Yes. They are. They had nothing to do with—"

"Have you a husband, Sarah? I was curious."

"Yes. I'm trying to reach a friend's farm and maybe he'll find me there."

"Does he love you—to let you go around the countryside like this?"

"He was away the Night of the War. He must have tried to get back. I know he's searching for us. I've met a man who told me—that John was still alive—was looking for us."

"John—a sturdy name." He smiled. "It is my name—in Russian, of course. Ivan. This John—you love him?"

"Yes," she answered.

"Then there is nothing I can do." He smiled.

"Major, I didn't—"

"You have a gun under your right thigh. You would shoot me?"

"If I had to," she said, surprised at the firmness of her voice.

"Then you are stronger than I am. I could bring you no harm. What is the Americanism—we are even, now?" He turned and called out something Russian. Almost immediately, the ranks of men in front of her blocking the truck, blocking her escape, began to fan apart.

"You're letting me—"

"Yes. Am I not stupid, though?" He smiled.

"I don't even know your na—"

"Maj. Ivan Borozeni, madam . . . Sarah. Literally, at your service." He stepped farther back from the truck and saluted her. "One fighter to another, then. And what is the expression? Godspeed—you and the children."

Sarah looked at him a moment, then whispered, so that only he could hear it, "I'll pray for you."

Borozeni nodded, then smiled. "And I, you, madam."

Sarah popped the clutch and started the truck ahead; she was crying.

Chapter 32

Ishmael Varakov stepped from the back of his limousine to walk across the airport runway surface. The V-STOL aircraft's engines were maddeningly loud, his feet ached and his belly felt constrained with his uniform blouse buttoned.

He walked toward a dark blue Cadillac, stopping for an instant to glance once again at the V-STOL aircraft. He watched as the remainder of the cargo was put aboard—Natalia's things.

He started walking again, stopping beside the rear door of the Cadillac, the driver—an Army corporal—saluting, Varakov returning it. The driver opened the rear door on the driver's side and as Varakov stepped inside, he looked at the man. "Go talk with my driver—about women or something." Varakov slammed the door shut behind him.

In the far corner of the back seat, looking frightened for the first time since he had seen her last as a little girl, sat Natalia Tiemerovna. Next to her—between himself and her—sat a young man, about Natalia's own age, but already with dark thinning hair above a high forehead. He wore glasses, wire-rimmed, and as Varakov settled his

179

bulk in the seat beside him, the young man pushed the glasses off the bridge of his nose.

"What the hell do you want with me?"

"Impertinent young man, aren't you?" Varakov smiled. "Here—if you promise not to shoot me with it yet." Varakov reached into his briefcase and took out the worn Browning High Power that belonged to Rubenstein. He rammed the magazine up the magazine well, then snapped back the slide of the pistol. He lowered the hammer over the loaded chamber and handed the pistol into Rubenstein's hands, which were opening and closing, balling in and out of fists.

"I told you," Natalia murmured. "My uncle is a man to trust . . . not to—"

Rubenstein looked at her and she fell silent. Then he turned to Varakov. "What do you want—General?" The younger man almost spat the word.

"You don't like Russians—let me guess. But you like Natalia, my niece. Doesn't that strike you as odd, young man?"

"I know her and—"

"You would be a terrible debater. It would then follow that once you got to know me, you would like me, wouldn't it? Logically, I mean?" Varakov felt himself smile.

Natalia laughed, a little laugh. Varakov liked her voice. It reminded him at times of that of her mother. "Well, will you listen to me, young man? For I need your help. Natalia needs your help; she doesn't know it yet. She is leaving here—for an extended stay."

"Uncle?"

"I had Catherine pack your things; they are aboard

that aircraft out there." Varakov gestured behind him. "Everything." Varakov looked at Rubenstein, then past him at Natalia. "You are both so young. It is the young who always risk for the errors of the old—like me. I have learned something of paramount importance—to your friend John Rourke, something which I must discuss with John Rourke in person. It is of importance to him and—"

"I'm not bringing John into a trap," Rubenstein snapped, his right fist tightening on the butt of the pistol he held.

"Two questions. Would Natalia knowingly do Rourke harm?"

"Of course not," Rubenstein told him.

"And would I, if I were planning to deceive both my niece and Rourke, entrust Natalia to him, through you? Obviously not. That is why she goes with you—for that reason and for her own safety."

"My safety . . ." Natalia began. "But—"

"You asked no questions when I sent you to explore Rozhdestvenskiy's office."

"Roz—what?" Rubenstein asked.

"Rozhdestvenskiy, a singularly good-looking fellow, yet singularly unpleasant, I am afraid." Varakov looked outside the window, watching his driver and the driver who had brought Natalia and Rubenstein, talking; he wondered about what. "I need you, Mr. Rubenstein, to take Natalia, my niece, to wherever it is John Rourke lives—"

"The Re—"

"The Retreat? Yes. I believe that's the place. Then,"— and Varakov fished inside his case—"you will give him this message. I am also giving you papers of safe conduct, for yourself and for Rourke, but I cannot guarantee how long my orders in such matters will be strictly enforced."

"Uncle," Natalia began.

"Silence, child." He looked at Rubenstein. "Can I entrust to you, sir, the one thing in my own life I hold most dear—her life?" Varakov extended his hand.

Rubenstein hesitated a moment, glanced at Natalia, then took Varakov's hand. "What the hell is going on here?"

"See? I told you you would like me, young man; I told you."

He started out of the back seat, opening the door, hearing Natalia's voice behind him as he exited the car.

"Uncle!"

She ran around the back of the car, then came into his arms. "I would not have let you go without saying goodby, child. I will see you again. Do not fear."

"What is happening, Uncle Ishmael? What is . . . that report of Rozhdestvenskiy, the Eden Project abstract?"

"Be thankful you read no more of it. You will learn the details when you come back here with John Rourke. There is no other way."

"Come back here with—"

"You must, child—and when Rourke reads the letter I have sent him, he will want to come. If he is the man I think he is—that you think he is . . . he is the only one." Varakov stepped back, holding his niece at arms' length. "You look lovely—a beautiful dress; that coat—real fur?"

"Yes." She looked down.

"I fear where you are going you'll have to change

aboard the aircraft. I know little about survival retreats, but I don't imagine one reaches them in high heels and silk stockings."

"They are nylon—silk stockings are—"

"Yes. Nylon. Be careful." He folded his arms around her. There was a possibility, he knew, that he would never see her again.

Chapter 33

The noise of the rotor blades was uncomfortable, despite the protective muffs on his ears, and there was always the distraction of the radio chatter coming from other ships in the squadron. But he didn't wish to turn it off.

Rozhdestvenskiy looked at the ground beneath him, the shadows there. Could Bevington, Kentucky, be far away? Could glory be much farther?

He reviewed the plan. Land the small armada in Bevington, Kentucky. Ground troops from . . . The name of the officer? Major Borozeni. Ground troops from Borozeni close into the valley. Locate Morris Industries. Empty the factory and load the equipment aboard the cargo helicopters coming from the west.

"Pilot, how long until we reach the staging area for the rendezvous with ground forces?"

"Twenty-three minutes, Comrade Major Rozhdestvenskiy."

"Twenty-three minutes," Rozhdestvenskiy repeated. The staging area, then Bevington, then glory—and then life, all but eternal.

He leaned slightly back in his seat. He was perfect for the role, he thought; he had always looked the part of a hero of the Soviet Union.

Chapter 34

Rourke opened his eyes, his breathing easier, his muscles aching, his body tired.

When he tried to move his arms, he could feel the aches in his forearm muscles. "Muscle relaxant," he whispered.

He tried to move his head; it raised, and he felt the dizziness, the light-headedness. "Morphine," he rasped, coughing. He remembered. Martha Bogen had given him the muscle-relaxant block, and reduced the shot of morphine. Death—because he couldn't have breathed.

He assumed he had awakened earlier than the other times—had he? He doubted his own ability to gauge time. He started to move his feet, his bound ankles, to flex his knees up. There was pain in his muscles, stiffness; he needed the pain and he moved his legs more, twisting his aching head from side to side, his neck hurting as he did. He breathed deeply—but not too deeply. He couldn't afford to pass out again, not with this his only chance.

It was as though, he realized, he were watching himself from a distance. His mind was clear enough—though holding a long train of thought was difficult. But his body was what seemed drunk, uncoordinated. He had stepped outside of himself, he felt. He started moving his arms up from his abdomen and chest and into the airspace above his head.

He heard the door, the key being turned, the woman coming.

"No—too soon," he rasped, thick-tongued, his voice sounding odd to him.

He could see her, coming toward him, the little black leather case in her hands.

"John, looking much better. I think I'll have to give you the full shot of the morphine this time or else you'll get out of hand. We wouldn't want that." She smiled as she bent over him, the needle in her right hand.

She squirted a little into the air, then lowered the needle toward him.

He slammed up his knees toward her stomach, both his fists bunched together and hammering against the right side of her head.

There was a short gasp like a scream and she disappeared below the level of the cot. He rolled over, half-falling on top of her. He raised his hands to break her exposed neck; but sank forward instead, across her body, the rope tightening around his neck.

He closed his eyes. . . .

He had to urinate. He opened his eyes. She would have been evacuating him, he realized. She? He looked under him; Martha Bogen was stirring but still unconscious.

Now able to remove the clothesline wrapped tightly around his neck, Rourke rolled away, pushing himself up on his hands to his knees. He rocked on his haunches for a long moment. He shook his head. "Morphine," he rasped. He tried pushing against the floor to get his feet under him, but fell flat onto the concrete.

He couldn't stand.

He looked up. There was a paper cutter in the far end of the library basement. Using his hands to pull himself, and his knees to push, he crawled toward it.

It seemed too far; he wanted to close his eyes. "Narcan," he murmured again. The morphine was taking hold.

She would have the Narcan to counteract it. "Antagonist," he murmured. Narcan was the antagonist for morphine.

"Paper cutter." He looked up. It was on the small table above him. He rolled the full weight of his body against it; the table turned over, the paper cutter clanging to the floor, the blade partially opened. He dragged himself toward it. Rourke reached out his wrists toward the blade and began to saw at the ropes. . . .

Naked, he sat on the floor; his body smelled of soap. She had apparently bathed him, he realized. He tried standing, getting to his feet, falling forward but catching himself on the end of the cot. Martha Bogen was murmuring something now, starting to come around. The basement door was unlocked; he remembered that it should be.

Where was the key? He could lock her inside.

He dropped to his knees, picking up the small leather case in his thick-feeling fingers. "Narcan," he murmured seeing the hypodermic needle. He hoped it was Narcan—not something else.

He took the syringe; he wanted a vein for the fastest action possible. He plunged the needle into his flesh. He started counting the seconds. It should take—how many? He tried to remember. Thirty—thirty seconds or so before he felt it. Rourke dropped the needle and slumped back on the cot, nausea and cold flooding over him as he closed his eyes. . . .

Rourke opened his eyes to see Martha Bogen, her hair mussed, her face bruised. standing over him, a needle in her right hand held like a dagger.

"No!" Rourke punched his right fist upward into her jaw. He sat up, his back aching, but his hands reaching out to catch the unconscious woman before she hit the concrete floor.

He swept her up into his arms, staggering for a moment under the added weight.

He walked the step toward the cot and, heavily, set her down.

"Martha," he murmured. He still had to urinate. He looked around the basement. There was a small door and he walked toward it, opened it—a bathroom. He stepped inside and relieved himself.

He felt the cold and the nausea coming. "Narcan— more Narcan," he murmured, already staggering. He reached the cot, found the package of syringes, opened the small leather case and took a fresh syringe.

He squatted on the floor, controlling his breathing so the Narcan wouldn't make him pass out. It shouldn't have been that way, he realized. It wasn't the Narcan, but the build-up of morphine in his system. He carefully found a spot and gave himself the injection, watching as the liquid dropped along the scale markings beneath the finger flange. Removing the needle, he sat quietly for a moment, feeling the dizziness start to subside.

He waited what he judged to be a full five minutes,

then tried getting to his feet.

Unsteady—but he could stand. He walked over to the small kit. There was one more syringe of Narcan. He closed the kit and took it with him as he started—shakily—toward the basement door. The thought occurred to him—break the blade off the paper cutter, in case more crazies were outside, waiting.

He didn't.

Rourke opened the door, then stepped through. The stairs were dimly lit, a stronger light glowing from the top. He leaned heavily against the wall of the stairwell as he started up, tired still, his muscles aching.

"B complex," he murmured. If he could reach his bike, he could give himself an injection. Another injection. "Shit," he murmured.

He reached the top of the stairs, the library empty through the open door, a light under a green shade glowing from the glass-partitioned office.

He lurched toward it, knocking over a large dictionary stand. He glanced back at it, then stood up straight, catching his breath. He reached the glass partition, then turned the knob of her office door. There was a small closet at the back, behind her desk.

As he opened the door, he started to feel his strength returning. Inside, neatly folded on the top shelf, were his clothes. He looked below. On the floor were his boots. No guns.

He turned to the desk, opening the large side drawer on the left-hand pedestal bottom.

The double Alessi shoulder rig, the twin Detonics stainless .45s. His A.G. Russell Sting IA knife.

He took up the shoulder rig, snapping one of the pistols out of the holster, then checked it—the chamber was still loaded, five rounds still in the magazine. He looked up; Martha Bogen was coming toward him.

He pointed the gun at her face. She stopped, then dropped to her knees on the floor and began to cry. "I didn't want to die alone."

"Nobody'll have to die; I won't let it happen."

"You can't stop it. You'll die, too. But we'll both die alone."

Rourke heard a tiny explosion, then a whistling sound. He glanced at his Rolex, still running in the drawer; then he pulled open the curtain over the window to the street. Against the darkness, he could see a skyrocket bursting. It was exquisite.

"I told you." He heard Martha Bogen's voice shout hysterically. "I told you so, John!"

The fireworks. Rourke remembered her saying they would come just before the explosions, just before the end.

Chapter 35

The pickup truck had thrown a part from the engine—she wasn't sure what—and the radiator had burst and the pickup had stopped dead.

For the last three miles, as she judged it, she and the children had walked hugging the side of the farm road—she had been too tired to cross country. With her, she carried the stolen M-16 rifle, her husband's .45—the gun now covered with a light layer of brown that she considered to be rust—and among her few personal effects the photographs she had taken from the farmhouse on the Night of the War. Her wedding picture with John was among them.

She sat staring at it now, folded, creased, cracked. He wore a tuxedo and she a floor-length white gown and a veil. The children were resting. It was not far to the Mulliner farm now, but they had needed to rest. She felt as though she were entering a new stage of her life, and somehow staring at the wedding photo had seemed necessary before going to the farm.

She put it away, seeing the picture more clearly in her mind than in the photograph. She remembered their wedding night, John's body next to hers—

"Mamma?"

She turned and looked at Michael in the predawn grayness. "Yes, son?"

"Will Daddy find us here—at Mary's?"

"I think so—if anyone can find anyone, Daddy will find us. Come here, Annie." Annie came beside her and Sarah hugged both children to her body.

She heard the barking of a dog, released the children, and grabbed for the rifle. But the dog stopped on the rise of ground, a golden retriever—the one her children had run with, played with. The dog ran up to them. Michael, and then Annie—always a little more afraid of dogs—hugged the animal, and were in turn licked in the face.

Sarah stood up, slinging the rifle across her back—she could rest now, at least until John found them. "Until," she repeated aloud.

Chapter 36

Natalia placed her hands on her waist, just above the Safariland holsters carrying the twin Smith & Wesson revolvers. She looked at Paul Rubenstein, saying, "I don't see anything, Paul."

"When John brought me up here the first time, he told me that was the whole idea." Rubenstein smiled in the gray predawn. "I can't really explain it as he does—but I guess he did a lot of research. He said it was the way Egyptian tombs were sealed, and things like that. He wanted the place tamper-proof. Watch this." Rubenstein approached a large boulder on his right. He pushed against it, and the boulder rolled away.

He walked to his left, pushing a similar but not identical boulder. It was more squared off. As Rubenstein pushed, the rock on which Natalia stood beside him began to drop down. As the rock beneath them dropped, a slab of rock—she compared it to a garage door—opened inward.

"John told me it's just a system of weights and counterbalances," Rubenstein told her. "Maybe you understand it better—didn't you have some training as an engineer?"

"Nothing like this," she said, feeling literally amazed.

Rubenstein shined a flashlight—she remembered it as one of the angleheads he and John had said they'd taken from the geological supply house in Albuquerque just after the Night of the War. In the shaft of yellow light, she could see Paul bending over, flicking a switch. The interior beyond the moved-aside slab of rock was bathed in red light now. "All ready for Christmas." Rubenstein laughed. "Red light? That was a joke."

"Yes, Paul," Natalia murmured.

"I'll get the bike. Hold this." He handed her the flashlight.

She studied the rock, murmuring, "Granite," as she heard the sounds of Rubenstein's Harley Low Rider being brought inside.

"Now watch this," Rubenstein said, suddenly beside her.

"Yes, Paul." She nodded, giving him back the flashlight. He moved over beside a light switch, then shifted a red-handled lever downward, locking it under a notch. He left the small cave for an instant and she could both hear and see him rolling the rock counterbalances back in place outside. Rubenstein returned to the red-handled lever, loosed it from the notch that had retained it, and raised it. The granite slab—the door—started shifting back into place, blocking the entrance.

"What are those steel doors for?" Natalia asked, gesturing beyond the pale of red light.

"The entrance inside." Rubenstein moved toward the doors, then began working a combination dial, then another, all in the shaft of yellow light from the anglehead. "John installed ultrasonic equipment to keep insects and critters out—"

"And closed-circuit television," Natalia added, looking up toward the vaulted rock above her.

"Can you find that switch for the red light back there?" Rubenstein asked her.

"Yes, Paul," she nodded, in the dim light found the switch, then worked it off. There was near total darkness now. "Paul?"

"Right here—wait." She heard the sounds of the steel doors opening.

She stepped closer to the beam of the anglehead flashlight, staring into the darkness beyond it.

"Ya ready?" she heard Paul's voice ask.

"I don't know . . . for—" She heard the sound of a light switch clicking.

She closed her eyes against the light a moment, then opened them.

"I don't believe it." She heard her voice; she couldn't remember it having ever sounded quite so astonished to her.

"That's the Great Room." She looked at Paul, watched the pride and happiness in his face.

"Great—yes," she repeated.

She started to walk, down the three low steps in front of her, a ramp to her left, her eyes riveted on the waterfall and the pool it made at the far end of the cavern; then she drifted to the couch, the tables, the chairs, the video recording equipment, the books that lined the walls, the weapons cabinet.

And on the end table beside the sofa . . . She stopped, approaching the couch, picking up the picture frame there.

"Would you like a drink, Natalia?" Rubenstein's voice came to her from across the Great Room. "I can show the rest to you after a while."

"What? A drink—yes," she called back.

The little boy in the photo—he was a miniature twin of John Rourke. "Michael," Natalia murmured, feeling herself smile. So fine, so beautiful, so strong. And the little girl—the face of an imp, a smile that— Natalia felt herself smiling more broadly.

And John, his arm around a woman who looked about Natalia's age, perhaps older by a few years. She was pretty, with dark hair and green eyes, or so it seemed in the picture.

"Sarah Rourke," Natalia murmured.

"That's them," Rubenstein said, suddenly beside her. "I didn't ask what you wanted. Figured Seagram's Seven would be all—"

"Perfect. That's perfect, Paul."

"That's Sarah and Michael and Annie. I feel almost as though I know them." Rubenstein laughed.

"Yes, Paul—so do I," Natalia said, putting the picture down on the end table. "So do I." She stopped talking then, because she felt she was going to cry and didn't want to.

Chapter 37

Rozhdestvenskiy looked at the Army major, Ivan Borozeni. "Major—it is immaterial to me if the population is unarmed essentially."

"But, Colonel, I see little need for going in firing—we—"

"Major, I will remind you of your rank—and also of one salient point you may not have considered. The Morris Industries plant was a highly secret Defense Department installation and manufacturing facility. If it still stands, it would seem obvious that the civilian government of the town is aware of its strategic importance to one degree or another. Hence, if we do not put down any thought of resistance as we enter the valley, they will likely use demolitions to destroy the plant."

"But, Comrade Colonel—"

Rozhdestvenskiy dragged heavily on his cigarette. "Your objections shall be noted in my official report. Now—lead your men into the assault."

The Army major stiffened visibly, then saluted, Rozhdestvenskiy, still dressed in civilian clothes, nodding only.

Rozhdestvenskiy turned and started back toward his command helicopter. In the far distance, he had been seeing fireworks illuminating the dawn sky. Peculiar, he had thought, surprised that Major Borozeni hadn't mentioned it. . . .

Below him now, he could see the helicopter gunships' shadows hovering like huge black wasps over the lip of the dish-shaped mountain valley, and beyond the rim, the first of Borozeni's attack forces were moving up. It was like a gigantic board game, he thought—this thing of being a field commander. He rather liked it.

Rozhdestvenskiy spoke into the small microphone in front of his lips. "This is Colonel Nehemiah Rozhdestvenskiy; the attack has begun!"

His jaw tightened, his neck tensed, and he nodded to his pilot, watching the man's hands as he worked the controls, feeling the emotion already in the pit of his stomach. They were starting down.

The mists on the ground rolled under the downdrafts of the helicopter rotors—he watched them swirl beneath the long shadow of his machine as they came from the sun. Surprise—there would be surprise, he thought.

Already, he could see the factory looming ahead and below them, the only large industrial building in the town, at its far edge.

"Down there," he rasped into his headset microphone. "There—get us down there." Then he switched channels, into the all-bands monitoring system so both Borozeni's ground commanders and the pilots of the other helicopter gunships could hear him. "This is Rozhdestvenskiy—we will converge on the factory due west of the town. Only KGB personnel will be allowed inside the factory complex itself, and only those with a clearance level over CX Seven will be allowed within the factory. Crush any resistance." He glanced through the bubble in front of him as another skyrocket soared up, exploding, as if the fools—he thought—were celebrating the attack. Into the microphone again, he snapped, "And find the source of those fireworks; I want them stopped!"

As he judged it, the factory was less than a mile away now so again he spoke into the microphone, but on the aerial-force band only. "This is Rozhdestvenskiy. Commando squad ready! Pilots take up positions!"

His own ship was hanging back as a half-dozen helicopter gunships, their cargo doors open, formed themselves into a crude circle around the factory fence, perhaps one hundred feet in the air.

Rozhdestvenskiy saw the first of the ropes being let down; then suddenly, like dozens of spiders sliding on filaments of web, dark-clad forms started down the ropes, rappelling toward the ground. "Good man!" he rasped, unconscious that he had spoken into the microphone.

The first of the men were on the ground, establishing a perimeter, their assault rifles and light machine guns ready.

The last of the commando team was down. "Move out, commando force ships," he barked into the microphone. "Take up positions two hundred yards from and around the factory fences."

Rozhdestvenskiy turned to his own pilot, tapping the man on the arm, then jerking his thumb downward.

The pilot nodded, then started the machine ahead and down.

Rozhdestvenskiy's mouth was dry, his palms sweating. He snapped up the collar of his windbreaker, checking the AKM across his lap.

He had never been in mass combat before.

The helicopter gunship was hovering, then dropping, gliding forward slightly and stopping.

He felt the lurch, felt the impact; then he released the restraint harness, throwing open the side door and stepping out near a squad of the commandos already on the ground, his own personal KGB team surrounding him.

"We enter the factory. Follow me!" He started to run, remembering as he ran to raise the rifle into an assault position.

The gates of the factory complex were locked with a chain, a massive padlock securing them.

"Stand back." He raised the assault rifle, firing into the lock. The sound of the jacketed slugs tearing into the metal of the lock was deafening, but the lock seemed to have been broken.

He reached for it, feeling the heat of the metal despite the gloves he wore, wrenching it open, then twisting it free of the chain.

"Get the gates opened—now!"

The chain-link twelve-foot gates swung inward, and Rozhdestvenskiy stepped into the service drive of Morris Industries—a giant step, he felt, in history.

He started to run, shouting again, "Follow me!" Above him, there was a spectacular burst, a skyrocket of blue and red and gold in a starburst, massive, exquisite.

He continued running, reaching a set of double doors. They would be locked. He raised the assault rifle again, firing into the locking mechanism. A burglar alarm sounded.

"Idiots," he shouted, then reached the doors, twisting

on the outside handle, wrenching the door open outward. He stepped into the factory complex, his men surrounding him. The building was in reality a series of interconnecting buildings.

"The loading docks," he shouted, then started running. If the materials he sought would be anywhere, they would be by the loading docks. There would be time then to search out precisely where they were manufactured. Gray light shafted through wire mesh-reinforced glass windowpanes as he ran the length of the first building; and occasionally through one of the windows as he looked out, he could see fireworks in the sky—more rockets, more starbursts. Were the people here insane?

He reached the end of a long corridor, already breathless from the running. Glancing to right and then to left, he looked right again. "There—hurry." For some reason, some reason he couldn't understand, he felt the need to hurry that much greater each time one of the skyrockets would explode. He felt—he couldn't define it.

Ahead of him he saw massive garage doors of corrugated metal, and between the doors and the corridor through which he ran, he could see crates—coffin-shaped and roughly the same size. He stopped running, leaning heavily against the wall, his breath coming in short gasps.

"Victory," he shouted. "The final victory over the Americans!" Suddenly the glass from the wire-meshed corridor windows shattered over his head, shards of it falling on and around him.

He stepped away from the wall, looking through the corridor windows into the dawning sky—a huge starburst, the largest firework he had ever seen—pale colors against a pale sky. And the concrete beneath him began to tremble, the walls to shake, dust and infinitesimally small chunks of debris drifting down.

"My God!" Where had he learned that? he thought. "They're blowing it up!" He started to run, the crates—the precious crates—behind him. Survival was more immediate now as the cross supports began crumbling and a three-foot section of concrete killed the commando beside him—just beside him.

Chapter 38

Squads of assault rifle-armed Soviet infantrymen were pouring through the streets.

"Damn it," Rourke rasped, both of the twin Detonics stainless .45s in his fists. Suddenly, the ground beneath him began to rumble, to shake.

He glanced at the black luminous face of the Rolex Submariner on his left wrist, then squinted skyward—full dawn. The explosions had begun just as Martha Bogen had said they would.

There was no time now—no chance to save the town. Russian troops—why?

The explosions. Already, in the distance near the high peaks of the rim of the valley, he could see rock slides starting.

He had waited near the school, still several blocks from Martha Bogen's house—and the garage where his Harley should still be hidden.

But waiting for the Soviet troops to clear the street in front of him would be suicidal now.

Thumb-cocking both pistols, he started to run, the ground shaking beneath him still more violently.

Gunfire. Soviet AK series assault rifles, firing toward

him, glass shattering in the louvered classroom windows beside him as he jumped a hedgerow, running.

Rourke wheeled beside a concrete vertical support for a portico roof. He fired the pistol in his right hand, then the pistol in his left, bringing down an assault rifle-armed soldier. The man's body spun, his assault rifle firing wildly, into his own men.

Rourke started to run again. Past a flagpole. During the day there would have been an American flag there and a Kentucky state flag as well.

He was nearly to the street beyond the school front lot. The ground trembled again.

He tried envisioning what the men and women of the town would have done to ensure their mass suicide. The ground trembled again and he saw a black disk sail skyward out of the street. There had been a large natural-gas storage area. . . .

"Natural gas," he rasped, throwing himself to the grassy ground beneath him.

The gunfire, the shouts, the commands in Russian and in English to halt—all were drowned out. Rourke dropped his pistols, covering his ears with his hands.

The street a hundred yards ahead of him was a sea of flame, chunks of paving hurtling skyward. They had mined the gas system.

Rourke grabbed for his pistols, pushing himself to his feet, running, stumbling, running again. A line of explosions—smaller ones—ripped through the road ahead of him in series. He had to cross the road to reach Martha Bogen's house on the other side.

He ran, bending into the run, arms distended at his sides. The gunfire resumed from behind him; he couldn't hear it, but could see the grass and dirt near his feet

204

chewing up under it.

He hit the pavement, still running, the explosions gutting the road drawing closer. Debris—bits of tarmac and cement and gravel—rained down on him. His hands, the pistols still in them, were over his head to protect it.

The road was now twenty-five yards away; his body ached; the waves of nausea and cold were starting to take hold.

"Narcan," he rasped. He needed the Narcan shot. He tripped, sprawling, pushed himself up, then ran on.

Ten yards. He was feeling faint, sick, the morphine was taking hold of him again.

Five yards. He jumped, the street ripping as a manhole cover less than a dozen yards to his right sailed skyward, roaring up on a tongue of flame. The street behind him exploded and he was thrown forward.

Rourke rolled, still clutching his pistols.

He started to his knees, hearing—not hearing but feeling—something behind him.

He wheeled, hitting the road surface, firing both pistols simultaneously. Two Soviet troopers fired at him; the ground beside him erupted under the impact of their slugs, both men going down under the impact of his.

He stumbled to his feet, lurching, feeling as though he would black out.

Rourke rammed both pistols, cocked and locked, into his wide trouser belt, then snatched at the injection kit inside his shirt against his skin. His hands shook, cold and nausea making his head reel. He dropped to his knees. The Narcan injection was in his right hand.

He looked beyond his hand as he tested the syringe.

"Man with a gun—Russian," he rasped, telling himself to act, forcing his body to respond. His left hand—he could feel the slowness—found the butt of one of his pistols. Automatically, he swept the left thumb around behind the tang of the Detonics to reach for the safety on the left side of the frame. He worked it down as the Russian soldier raised his assault rifle.

Rourke's right hand worked toward his left arm, the sleeve pulled up already—he had planned ahead as he always did.

He started raising his left arm, as if both sides of his brain were taking separate control of him. He tried squinting at the sights a moment, seeing the hypodermic come into his line of fire.

His right hand jabbed the hypo into his left forearm.

"Aagh," he shouted, feeling the change sweep over him, seeing the slow-motion movement in his left hand as the thumb moved back around the tang, out of the way of the slide.

He was suddenly back—cold and sweating, but back, his mind working. His left first finger worked the trigger and the Detonics bucked hard in his hand.

The Soviet trooper's assault rifle fired skyward as his body twisted, almost as in a dance, then crumpled to the roadside.

Rourke pushed himself to his feet. That had been the last Narcan shot, but the last he should need. He snatched at the other pistol in his belt, worked down the safety and—he could not run again—he started into a loping walk to the curb.

Rourke assessed his surroundings—head left. He started that way. It was at least another block, maybe two. The B-complex shot would start working soon after he administered it—after he got to it.

The nausea was passing, the coldness subsiding; his

head ached and his muscles ached.

As he increased his stride, more explosions rocked the ground beneath him. Glass, in windows on both sides of the street he loped into, shattered; fires erupted everywhere.

Another manhole cover sailed skyward on a column of flame and Rourke jumped away, the explosion ringing in his ears, debris falling like rain on him.

He rolled onto his back, protecting his face with his left forearm.

He had to run. He rolled onto his knees, then pushed himself up, starting forward, lurching into a ragged, long-strided run.

More gunfire behind him. He wheeled, almost losing his balance. He pumped a shot at hip level with the Detonics in his right fist, downing a Soviet soldier at the end of the block.

He turned and kept running.

He could see the house—white frame with green vines growing up the round columns on the front porch. Rourke could see the driveway; his bike would be in the garage at the end of it.

Still running, he glanced behind him. No one. Perhaps the Russians were getting out while they still could.

More explosions. Rourke glanced up, toward the rim of the valley; rock slides were everywhere, the very faces of the peaks changing, seeming to melt away.

Rourke turned up the driveway, running harder now, sweating. The garage door—ten yards, five . . . He stopped. It would be locked. He raised both pistols, firing the one in his right hand, then the one in his left. The garage-door lock shattered as he loped and lurched forward. He fell against the door.

Jamming the pistols into his belt, he wrenched the door handle, twisting it, shoving it up, letting the door slide out of sight.

The jet black Harley—he saw it. Rourke stumbled toward it. His gear looked untouched.

He snatched at the CAR-15 wrapped inside a blanket and a piece of ground cloth.

He ripped the covering away, then searched the musette bag slung on the handlebars. he found a thirty-round magazine, rammed it up the well, and eared back the bolt handle.

He let the bolt slide forward.

"Come on," he rasped, staring out into the street. He could hear the sounds of more explosions; the gas lines were still going, of their own accord now.

Rourke slung the CAR-15 cross-body from his left shoulder, under his right arm.

He started searching the Lowe pack and found his medical kit, the injection kit inside it. Rourke opened that, taking the B-complex syringes and jabbing one into his left forearm.

He dropped to his knees, trying to even his breath.

Chapter 39

Her jaw hurt where the man, John, had hit her. On her knees, on the window seat in the main room of the library overlooking the street and the post office beyond, she wrang a handkerchief in her hands, red hearts embroidered on it, a gift from her husband years ago.

There were fires all over the city; she was afraid of fire.

Everyone else was with someone, safe, ready to die. John was out there in the streets, somewhere. He wouldn't make it; she knew that. She had nursed for her husband often enough to know that in his condition, he would be too weak to travel far. She had never even told him the secret paths through the valley to reach beyond the mountains.

He would die alone; she would die alone.

She wondered what his last name was.

He hadn't hit her because he hated her. It was because he hadn't wanted to die with her.

"I hope you live, John," she said, suddenly feeling a weight slip from her.

The manhole cover in the street outside rocketed skyward, the flame under it rising, spreading. The floor under her shook; the plate-glass window in front of her shattered.

She had one more injection—one she had saved in her desk drawer.

It would make her sleep. She gave it to herself, letting the needle fall from her hand, her hands bloody from the glass that had cut her as the window shattered around her.

There was a cool wind and as she closed her eyes, she could see her dead husband's stern face. He was scolding her for what she had tried to do, but there was love in his eyes. . . .

Chapter 40

Rourke settled himself on the seat of the Harley, the motor purring under him, the tanks full, the Detonics stainless .45s reloaded and holstered in the Alessi rig across his shoulders. He was slightly cold—the exhaustion, the drugs coursing through his veins. The collar of his brown leather jacket was snapped up.

Under the jacket he carried the musette bag on his left side, spare magazines for the Detonics pistols and for the CAR-15 slung under his right arm.

On his right hip was the Python, Metalifed and Mag-Na-Ported; spare ammo for the big Colt was in the musette bag, too, in Safariland Speedloaders.

There were Soviet troops on the ground, Soviet helicopters in the air above. The ground beneath him trembled. Fire was everywhere—in the houses on both sides of the street, a wind whipping it up as he looked out of the garage.

He had been breathing, slowly, evenly, getting the house that was his body in order, summoning up the reserves of strength he would need.

It was that or die.

His left fist worked in the clutch, his right throttled

out, and the Harley started ahead.

With his right thumb he worked the CAR-15's safety off, then moved his left hand quickly, securing the dark-lensed aviator-style sunglasses.

He squinted through them as he braked in the middle of the street.

In an inside pocket of his leather jacket were some of his dark tobacco cigars.

He took one and placed it between his teeth, rolling it into the left corner of his mouth, unlit.

"Ready," he whispered to himself.

He throttled the Harley, working through the gears, lowering his frame across that of the bike, reaching the end of the street, making a sharp right, then accelerating again. In his mind's eye he could see the way he'd entered the town and that was the only way he knew to leave it.

He passed the post office. As he cut another left, into the street angling past the library, it was a sea of flames.

"Martha," he rasped, looking away as he gunned the jet black Harley ahead.

Despite it all, he felt a sadness for the woman.

Soviet troops on the right, two of them aflame from the gas fires, three of them wheeling toward him, started to fire their assault rifles. Rourke gave the Harley gas then shifted his grip to the CAR-15. Firing rapid two-round semiautomatic bursts, he nailed the nearest of the men, then the one behind him.

Gunfire from the third man's assault rifle ripped into the street surface beside him. Rourke throttled out, cutting a broad arc as he made a hard right, then angled off the street and into the grassy shoulder paralleling it. Fires still raged on the far side by the school building. Soviet troops ran haphazardly about, an officer in their midst; Rourke spotted him, a tall man, his hat gone, his face dirt-smudged.

There was an overturned jeep, and though the officer called to his men, they were scattering. The officer was tugging at something under the jeep.

Rourke sped past, glancing left, seeing a form half under the jeep, the officer working with a pry bar, trying to get someone out.

Rourke slowed the Harley, cutting a wide arc. The jeep was close to the fires raging down the center of the street; the grass on the far side of it was burning.

"Shit," Rourke rasped, gunning the Harley back toward the jeep.

The officer dropped the pry bar, snatching at a full-flap military holster on his right hip.

Rourke slowed the bike, stopping, the CAR-15 pointed straight at the Russian.

"Shoot me, then. But first help me get this man out; he's still alive!"

Rourke said nothing. His right thumb flicked the safety of the CAR-15 on, and he let down the Harley's stand, the engine cut off.

He walked toward the Russian, saying, "I'm ill—not as strong as I usually am. You work the pry bar; I'll pull him out."

"Agreed." The Soviet officer nodded.

The man—a major, Rourke noticed—leaned against the pry bar. Rourke dropped to his knees in the street beside the injured man pinned under the overturned jeep.

An older man—a senior noncom of some kind. The face, unconscious, was pleasant-looking.

Rourke grabbed the man's shoulders, "Now, Major," Rourke ordered, feeling the jeep rising slightly beside him, hearing the groaning as the Soviet officer strained on the pry bar. Rourke put his own right shoulder to the end of the overturned jeep, then threw his weight back, sprawling backward into the street with the older man, getting him clear as the jeep fell.

"I could not hold it anymore!"

Rourke ignored the officer, looking to the older man. "He's gonna need a hospital and quick."

"There are helicopters—cargo helicopters. They can be used for the wounded."

"You get him outa here fast," Rourke rasped. "This whole town's gonna blow."

"What are you doing?" The major's right hand went out to Rourke's right forearm.

Rourke shook it away, then opened the leather case which had Martha Bogen's shot kit.

"Morphine," Rourke rasped. "Relax. I'm a doctor. Put a compression bandage on that right leg—not a tourniquet unless you want him to lose it." Rourke pulled his knife, then cut at the noncom's sleeves, first the right, then the left, using one sleeve folded over as a bandage, the second to secure it to the leg. "Not too tight. Looks like you've got somebody to baby-sit with, Major." Rourke stood up.

The Soviet officer's right hand moved and Rourke started for his rifle, but the hand was extending toward him.

Rourke took it.

"I should arrest you—or have you shot."

"That last part"—Rourke smiled—"I was kinda thinkin' the same thing myself. But I'll pass on it."

Rourke loosed the Soviet major's hand and turned to walk away. There was a chance the man would pull a gun and shoot; Rourke decided he wasn't going to count it a possibility.

He stepped aboard the Harley, gunning the engine to life, letting up the kick stand.

The major was looking to his injured sergeant.

Rourke gunned the Harley ahead. . . .

He was at the end of the town now. Only the road leading up into the mountains and out of the valley was ahead.

Explosions rocked the ground under and around him, and behind him there was a growing fire storm, already edging into the wooded area around the town.

He looked at the town one more time—Bevington, Kentucky. "Sad," he murmured, then started the Harley up ahead.

The road was steep going; rock slides were starting to his right, his attention focusing there as he steered the Harley around boulders that had already strewn the road.

Overhead, above the thundering of the explosions and the hissing roar of the fire storm behind him, he heard a sound—familiar. He glanced skyward—helicopters.

"That's what I get for being a good Samaritan," he rasped, shaking his head. But he didn't blame the major, or the injured sergeant. Like most things in life, he thought, gunning the Harley on, the exhaust ripping under him and behind him, there was no one to blame.

The helicopters were clearly after him; he didn't know why. Maybe the KGB, he thought—but why had they been in Bevington, Kentucky, to begin with?

He swung the CAR-15 around, the safety off. There was a sharp bend in the road and Rourke took it at speed, cutting a sharp left onto the shoulder because half the width of the road was strewn with boulders. There was a rumbling sound to his left and Rourke looked that way— a rock slide, shale and boulders skidding down for as far as he could see, a rock slide paralleling the roadway.

"Shit," he rasped, glancing up at the helicopters. There was a chattering sound; he didn't have to look again. Machine-gun fire.

The road dipped, Rourke accelerating into the grade. The rock slide was coming inexorably closer, closer. The area to his right was heavily wooded; fire swept through it.

Rourke skidded the bike hard left, then right, avoiding a deer that ran from the flaming forest on his right. He accelerated, the rock slide still coming.

Machine-gun fire tore into the road beneath him, bullets ricocheting off the rocks to his left.

The road took a fast cut left and Rourke arced the Harley into it. As he hit the straightaway, he twisted in the Harley's saddle, the CAR-15—stock retracted— pointing skyward at the nearest of the helicopters. He let off a fast semiauto burst—six shots in all. The helicopter pilot pulled up.

Rourke let the rifle drop to his side on the sling, then throttled out the Harley, the rim of the valley in sight, perhaps a mile ahead.

Gravel and smaller rocks were pelting at him, hammering against the road surface, their effect almost indistinguishable from the machine-gun fire from the choppers above. The fire on his right was up to the roadside, and the trees flanking the road on his right were torches, columns of fire; the heat from them scorched at his skin as he drove his machine upward—toward the rim of the valley.

216

Massive boulders were falling now. Rourke steered the bike around them as they impacted on the road before him. A tree, still a mass of flames, fell; Rourke gunned the Harley full throttle, his body low over the handlebars, as he passed under it, burning branches and chips of bark spraying his hands, his face, his clothing.

Rourke squinted back, beyond the burning tree trunk and skyward. The helicopters were still coming.

He cut the Harley sharp left, taking the grade that would take him to the rim, boulders rolling across the road before him now, missing him by inches, the Harley's exhaust like a cannon, like a trumpet, strident, tearing at his eardrums, the wind of the slipstream lashing at him, hot from the fire raging to his right.

More machine-gun fire, the helicopters above him now, one of them ahead of him.

Rourke couldn't free a hand to shoot back. The very fabric of the mountains was crashing down toward him, dust and smoke in a cloud around him as he hit the rim.

Rourke skidded the bike into a tight turn, breaking, balancing the machine with his feet as he stopped it, telescoping the stock, then shouldering the CAR-15. There was no escape from the helicopters, as he had just escaped the rock slides and the fire storm.

He rammed a fresh thirty-round stick into the Colt and ripped away the scope covers, sighting on the nearest of the bubble domes as the helicopter closed with him, machine-gun bullets ripping into the dirt and rocks around him.

Chapter 41

"Come in, Colonel! Borozeni calling Colonel Rozhdestvenskiy. Come in. Ground to air . . . come in!"

There was no answer, then, "Major Borozeni . . . Lieutenant Tiflis calling Major Borozeni!"

"Come in, Tiflis, over."

"Comrade Major, we cannot contact Colonel Rozhdestvenskiy. . . . What are the orders? Over."

"Tiflis, bring your helicopters back." Tiflis had commanded the helicopter force, not the special gunship fleet that had brought in Rozhdestvenskiy's commando team for seizing the factory, but the medivac and cargo helicopters. "Tiflis, listen carefully. . . . Use your radio. . . . It's stronger. Contact the entire helicopter fleet. . . . I am assuming command in the apparent absence of Colonel Rozhdestvenskiy. Over."

"Yes, Comrade Major. Over."

"Tiflis." Borozeni remembered to work the push-to-talk button on his radio. "Tiflis, contact me on how many ships. . . . We have hundreds of wounded. . . . Hurry. Out."

"Tiflis out, Comrade Major."

There was only static. Borozeni glanced down to the

unconscious sergeant beside him. Borozeni's knee ached. He shifted position, but could not move his bloodstained right hand lest the bleeding increase. He assumed the man on the motorcycle really had been a doctor—or at least had known what he'd talked about. The shot of morphine had helped the sergeant.

"Tiflis to ground. Tiflis to ground command."

"Borozeni here. . . . What is it, Tiflis?"

"Tiflis to ground . . . All but four—repeat four, Comrade Major—all but four of the helicopters return-ing. . . . Landing will begin in two minutes. Tiflis over."

"We need them all. . . . What are they doing? Over."

"In pursuit of man riding motorcycle out of valley, Comrade Major . . . May be the American agent Rourke, wanted by KGB. Over."

Borozeni smiled. A man on a motorcycle. So his name was Rourke. "Tiflis, tell the commanders of those four ships to—"

"Tiflis out."

Borozeni worked the push-to-talk button, then stared skyward at the chopper. What had happened? "Tiflis to ground . . . Tiflis to ground . . . Over."

"What was the meaning of that? Borozeni over."

"Tiflis to ground . . . The suspected American agent just shot at the helicopters, Comrade Major. Over."

"Tell them to pull back . . . or I will personally have them on report to General Varakov. Borozeni out."

Borozeni smiled, murmuring in English, "Even."

Chapter 42

Rourke squeezed a single shot toward the dome of the nearest helicopter, the ground around him now erupting with the impact of the machine-gun fire from the four gunships.

Squinting through the three-power Colt scope, he could see the glass dome take the impact of the slug. Rourke fired again, the recoil hammering at his right shoulder, his arms almost too tired to hold up the gun. The glass spider-webbed again.

The four ships were circling him now. Rourke concentrated on the one he could bring down, taking aim for a third shot at the same area where the Plexiglass would be weakest.

Sarah. Michael. Annie. Paul would find them, care for them.

"Die," Rourke shouted at the helicopter. The machine swerved and his shot went wild, all four machines rising rapidly, hovering, and turning into a ragged formation, then disappearing back toward the valley.

Rourke let the rifle sink down.

He didn't believe in luck—but he didn't argue with it either. He worked the safety on for the Colt assault rifle, then gunned the Harley over the lip of the valley and down toward the highway. . . .

He had washed his body in an icy stream, and now—tired and changed into fresh clothes—he sat by his motorcycle, stirring cold water into a pack of his freeze-dried food. He tasted a spoonful of it. It would have been better hot, but the nutritional value was the same. He had added a hundred miles since leaving Bevington and was well inside Tennessee. Paul had probably passed him. Perhaps Paul had found them.

Rourke leaned back, eating his cold food, his muscles still aching, his stomach still uneasy. He planned ahead—always. He hadn't planned on Martha Bogen, or on the suicide of an entire town. Or on the Russians being there. The sun was setting—red on the horizon, too red, the weather warm now.

He had seen signs of Brigands in the last twenty-five miles—their habitually careless camps, litter and broken bottles everywhere.

To the east, he could see the faint glimmering of some early stars on the horizon.

Tomorrow, he would renew the search, to find Sarah, Michael, and Annie. And perhaps Paul really had found them.

He would stop at the Retreat, he decided.

He finished the food, then set the empty package aside. Finding a cigar in his shirt pocket, he lit it in the blue-yellow flame of his Zippo.

John Rourke made a last check of the twin Detonics

.45s, then of the CAR-15. He had cleaned all three guns, and reloaded the spare magazines for them.

As he watched the last wash of red in the sky where the sun was fast vanishing, he closed his eyes. Sarah, Michael, Annie. Paul Rubenstein.

Another face—her eyes were a brilliant blue.